CW00405745

Shade and Light

Also by Maryann D'Agincourt

Journal of Eva Morelli

All Most

Glimpses of Gauguin

Printz

Shade and Light

Maryann D'Agincourt

PP
Portmay Press
New York

Cover image: *Berkshire Community College Students*, Norman Rockwell (b. 1894, d. 1978), Graphite on paper, 1967, Norman Rockwell Museum Collections

Cover design by Emily Albarillo

Printed in the United States of America

First printing, 2018

ISBN: 978-0-9994006-1-6 (hc)

Library of Congress Control Number: 2018957715

Publisher's Cataloging-In-Publication Data
(Prepared by The Donohue Group, Inc.)

Names: D'Agincourt, Maryann, author.
Title: Shade and light / Maryann D'Agincourt.
Description: New York : Portmay Press, [2018] | Series: [Art fiction series] ; [book 5]
Identifiers: ISBN 9780999400616 (hardcover) | ISBN 9780999400630 (ebook)
Subjects: LCSH: Immigrant families--Massachusetts--Fiction. | World War, 1939-1945--Psychological aspects--Fiction. | Anti-fascist movements--Italy--Trieste--History--20th century--Fiction. | Artists--Massachusetts--Fiction. | Man-woman relationships--Fiction. | LCGFT: Historical fiction.
Classification: LCC PS3604.A332544 S53 2018 (print) | LCC PS3604.A332544 (ebook) | DDC 813/.6--dc23

Portmay Press
244 Madison Avenue
New York, NY 10016
www.portmaypress.com

In art, there is no need for color; I see only light and shade. Give me a crayon, and I will paint your portrait.
—Francisco de Goya

In memory of Josephine Coscia Reppucci, 1915–2007

For Gwyneth

Deepest gratitude to Emily Albarillo for her fine editing of this manuscript and her exquisite cover design

One

Encounters

Jonas Hoffman's parents had met in front of the Ethel Barrymore on an October evening, two months before the attack on Pearl Harbor. Moonlight flowed down Forty-Seventh Street, burnishing the lettering on the marquee. From opposite directions they each approached the theater.

On the trip to New York, Jonas's mother, Cora, then twenty years old, had been accompanied by her younger sister Rina. As the Arenzi family lived in close proximity to Boston, the sisters had taken the train from South Station to Penn Station to see the musical *Best Foot Forward*. David, Jonas's father, was alone; a few hours earlier a customer in his family's hardware store had offered him a free ticket to the play. Because of the vigorous wind that evening and the future Mr. and Mrs. Hoffman's attempts, heads lowered, to dodge the next anticipated gust, along with the disparity in their heights, they collided. Then, after collecting themselves, they each profusely apologized, while Rina, her shoulders sloping, waited near the door of the theater. When the play was over, Cora Arenzi and David Hoffman spoke again.

A concise version of the encounter was told to an eight-year-old Jonas on a Sunday afternoon in late 1953. He sat slouched in a large, soft armchair across from the vacant brick fireplace in his aunts' living room, the November rain pelting the windowpane. With a bored and dubious expression crossing his narrow face he toyed with the plastic figures of horses and cows Rina would present to him whenever he and his mother visited.

Fraternal twins, Rina and Belinda were five years younger and four inches taller than his mother—Rina had blond hair she wore upswept in a chignon, later a French twist; Belinda's dark fine locks fell unstyled to her waist. In contrast, his mother's chestnut brown hair was cut short and tucked behind her ears. Whenever a young Jonas would come upon Cora sleeping, he'd gingerly touch her hair; enticed by her beatific expression, he'd rub a few strands between his fingers, moved by how soft and wispy it felt.

While her two sisters smoked incessantly, Cora refused to touch a cigarette. Moments before they had come into the room, he had noticed a trail of cigarette smoke wafting from the kitchen, followed by the low and pressured voices of his mother and aunts.

Jonas's heart pounded; he sensed something of consequence was about to happen. He tightly clutched the white plastic horse in his right hand. When he looked up, Aunt Belinda was approaching. Her lips pursed, she knelt before his chair, her long hair grazing the armrest. Although she was the one Arenzi sister who had not been in New York that October evening twelve years before, she had been chosen to speak because, of the three, she was best able to contain her emotions; her speech was most to the point. She leaned in close, and as she spoke, he felt the pressure of her forefinger on his wrist. He was uneasy: no one but his mother had acknowledged his father's existence—it was a forbidden topic, he'd gleaned—and whenever Cora had done so she had spoken in a soft and somber tone about David's passing years before.

As he had never known his father, the young Jonas had no desire to learn how his parents had met. His sharp sense of color was what he would often refer to to help him interpret what he viewed as an intrusive and murky adult world. Half listening to his aunt's words, he became absorbed by his mother's royal blue skirt, the curvy hem, and how the material swung as she paced by the window, her arms akimbo, the shade half-drawn, the lower pane splattered with rain. Next, and with the same intense focus, he studied Aunt Belinda's purple V-neck sweater, his gaze lingering on the two cigarettes she had tucked inside her bra. Lastly, he fixed his eyes on Aunt Rina, standing in the far corner of the room, wearing a pale gray dress, soft and diaphanous, her face slightly flushed. It then came to him—he imagined his mother as a blue arc darting forward, Belinda a hovering and fierce purple wind, Rina a floating moon, and his father a large moving shadow.

After Belinda finished speaking, she rose, her mouth now relaxed, and caught his gaze. In the same direct way, she asked if he'd like ice cream. Within seconds, his aunts and mother had gone back into the kitchen; Jonas soon followed.

What he would most remember about that day would be the persistent sound of rain against the windowpane, the curve in the hem of his mother's skirt, and the cigarettes crushed between Belinda's breasts. He would carry no particular memory of Rina because she was and always would be the same to him—warm and elusive. It would be years before it would dawn on him that the intervention had occurred because his mother and aunts had been concerned—as of that day he had not asked any one of them about his father. For he had remained silent and still whenever his mother had spoken of David.

Over the years that followed, the circumstances of his father's death would become more and more clear to him. From conversations he had had with his mother at different stages in his life, he had pieced together that his father had died toward the end of World War II, two months after he had married his mother and five months prior to Jonas's birth. His father, during his training as a medic, had developed a mysterious infection a few days before he'd been scheduled to be sent overseas. He passed away three days later. It was difficult to imagine a strong, vibrant young man, as Jonas believed his father had been, becoming suddenly very ill. In his photos David Hoffman appeared tall, robust. In most of the pictures his father had posed in the same way, his hands pressing against his hips, his elbows spread out to the sides. If he had lived, Jonas imagined him striking the same pose if he'd done something his father approved of or if he'd done something that had displeased him—his father's chest more expansive in the former case and more concave in the latter. The only photo Jonas had seen of his father not posing with hands on hips was his wedding picture. When Jonas was about fourteen, he deduced that in this photo he was already growing inside of his mother and, with both angst and gratification, he realized it would be the only picture of the three of them together.

On those snowy weekends of his childhood his mother would appear less grounded, more ethereal, more similar in demeanor to Rina. In the small, wood-paneled den, Jonas would stand close to her and study how languorously yet precisely she'd iron a dress of hers or a shirt of his. Or in the kitchen he'd sit on a stool and observe her stirring flour and eggs together, her hips gently swaying. She'd speak about his father in a low singsong voice. "He was kind and sensitive," she'd say, her warm and intelligent brown eyes reflecting concern. Then, while collecting her thoughts, she'd momentarily raise the object in her hand—either a wooden spoon or an iron—before continuing. "Because of his kindness and sensitivity he had been rejected to a certain degree by his family. They were New Yorkers—their ancestors had come to America years and years ago, one hundred or more, I think. They'd been hoping for an ambitious son. But he was happy." And then she would smile, her lips closed, in that quick and thoughtful way of hers.

This had led to a recurring image of his father dressed in beige, lazily lying in a hammock with his eyes

6

shut, and yet Jonas felt uneasy viewing him in this way. He believed he had done so because he had found the meaning behind his mother's words obscure: "to a certain degree," "rejected," "ambitious," "New Yorkers." He was convinced there was more to what she was saying than he comprehended or she wanted revealed.

After a year or so of such conversations with his mother, which began when Jonas was about ten years old, he turned to his aunts for clarification. He did so on the day his class discussed their fathers' work. When it came to what he thought was his turn, Jonas stood up, his heart beat frantically, and he said, "World War II, he died." Everyone in the class turned to look at him in awe. Although they all knew his father had passed away during the war, they appeared to have a newfound respect for him now that he had boldly acknowledged it.

His teacher, a frenzied woman with dark unkempt hair and pointy glasses, looked confused for a moment; she had had no intention of calling on Jonas. She blushed and said, her voice weakening, "Thank you, Jonas. Your father was a hero." Reflexively Jonas smiled with hesitant pride, gazing back at the other students—he liked the word "hero"; it erased the image that previously had come to mind—no longer would he view his father as lethargic and unfocused, but energetic and larger than life—heroic.

Once school was dismissed he made his way to his aunts' home. It was a warm day in mid-June, and he found Aunt Rina sitting outside on the front steps, her palms grazing the concrete, a cigarette burning between two fingers, her long legs crossed, an open book over-turned next to her. She was looking off into the distance. Jonas knew she enjoyed conversing with Mr. O'Malley, who lived across the street, and assumed she was star-ing at his home, a red brick ranch with flagstone steps, hoping he would come over and strike up a conversation. She wore more makeup than usual, her eyeliner going beyond her eyes, giving her a theatrical look.

As Jonas approached, he waved his hand. He knew she had not noticed him coming up the walk.

Her tone easy, she said, "Handsome, you nearly scared me." He was encouraged, for he relished the sound of Aunt Rina's hushed voice.

"Are you waiting for him?" he asked, turning to look in the direction of the house across the street.

"I'm waiting for you, Jonas," she said defensively, her eyes on him. "How was your day?"

Her eyes peered into his; he felt a deep sense of comfort. Hastily she turned to snuff out her cigarette, and then cupped his chin in her hand, her long fingers enfolding his face, gazing at him in that penetrating yet elusive way of hers.

When she released his chin, he sat next to her and placed his homework folder down beside him, his hands pressed against the step. He stretched out his legs and crossed his ankles. The sun in his eyes, he squinted and told her what happened in school that day. Occasionally a car passed by. The sound of a lawn mower in the distance afforded him a sense of privacy. From time to time his gaze would stray across the street to see if Mr. O'Malley, who was a few inches shorter than his aunt, had come out of his home.

"Did you know him well?" he asked, feeling the words stick in his throat. It was the first time he had asked her about his father.

"Of course I knew David," she said with a distant look in her eyes. "He was shy and sweet and I thought Cora was lucky to have met someone like him."

"Was he a hero?"

Her eyes saddened, her voice even lower now, she answered, "Yes, he was a hero, he was heroic, he'd been that way since the day we met him." Brightening some, she continued, "Your mother and father were an attractive couple—sophisticated."

No longer fixated on the house across the street, her eyes wore a hurt expression.

Seven months later, on a cold, wintry day, he asked Belinda about his father. It was a snowy day in early

January and school had been canceled, but it was not stormy enough for his mother or Rina not to go into work. Jonas spent the day with Belinda, who was free on Mondays. Once finished with her chores, phone calls, and shopping—usually by the middle of the afternoon—she'd sit down with Jonas and read aloud from a novel by Mark Twain or Charles Dickens or James Fenimore Cooper. Her body hunched over, she'd enunciate with pinpoint accuracy, which Jonas often found more intriguing than the story.

On that day she held a copy of *A Tale of Two Cities* in her hand and was about to open it to the page she'd left off reading a few days before. Touching her arm, Jonas asked, his voice stoic, if she had known David. She paused and sat still, her fine dark hair sprawled across her narrow back. Turning to him, she met his gaze and spoke frankly: "Your father was a fine man, Jonas—kind, considerate, and truthful. He was an individual—well-read and intelligent. Your mother was content with him. They were a happy couple." Next she opened the book, lowered her head, and began to read in her careful and direct way. Although her eyes was steady and fixed on the page, he noticed a lone tear trickle unevenly down her cheek.

~

Jonas harbored two visions of what his parents had been like as a couple, gleaned from his mother's textured words about his father, and from what he had learned from Rina and Belinda. And then there was his own independent impression—what he had come to understand about his father from the grainy photograph he kept beneath his mattress. His father had been eighteen years old when the picture was taken. He stood with two other men of his age in front of what appeared to be a hardware store. Jonas thought he could make out the name "Hoffman" on the sign. He would pull the photograph out, hold it close to the light, and assiduously study it in bed each night.

One vision he had of his parents was of the two of them living in a big city with many skyscrapers, walking down a crowded street, holding hands, his mother's set expression emanating with passion and determination. His father's demeanor was quiet and humble as they passed through the crowd, nothing about them ruffled, their expressions not changing, a halo of contentment surrounding them amidst the throngs of people and light rain.

The other image he held of his parents was of them at an elaborate party, admired by people, involved in separate conversations, dressed elegantly, his father heroic-looking and debonair, his mother wearing makeup, dressed in a fitted red and gold shimmering gown, her shoes matching the colors of her dress, the heels narrow and high. They confidently conversed with others, and when those they happened to be speaking with didn't notice, they would steal a long and passionate glance at each other.

Given his doubting nature, Jonas lightly questioned his imaginings. Ultimately it did not matter to him whether or not they were true. In such instances he was not a stickler for veracity. He chose to conjure his parents in these ways because such thoughts buoyed him.

Jonas grew to view marriage as a complex mystery. His perspective was the natural consequence of having experienced his parents' union only within the realm of his imagination, one that filled his young mind with gauzy images of heroes and halos, rainy days and sophisticated parties. Whenever any one of those images began to fade, he would turn to the dictionary. With the heavy Webster in hand that his mother kept lying horizontally on the lowest shelf of the kitchen bookcase, he would climb into bed, his heart racing, and scroll his flashlight across the tiny printed definition in an attempt to seek out the true meaning of the word "marriage." Yet invariably it remained a dry and elusive concept for him.

He would sustain that viewpoint for many years not only because of the unions of those in his general purview, but because of his natural dubiety. Imbued, he supposed, with primarily an artistic temperament and not necessarily a psychological one, in the case of marriage he could not penetrate what was happening beneath the surface of any relationship—all appeared to seesaw unnervingly from banality to excitement. And he, Jonas Hoffman, was the skeptical albeit determined onlooker observing the ups and downs of every union he witnessed.

In his twenties, Jonas would come to know Jenny Smila, a seemingly shy woman of eighteen. He'd often wonder if her shyness was a mask of sorts, not a simple black or white plastic one, but a colorful and intricate papier-mâché mask decorated with rich fabrics and jewels, one that could be found in shops along the narrow cobblestone streets of Venice. It was a mask she wore with much subtlety and ease as if indeed it were a simple plastic one, an item that at her discretion she could gracefully slip on and off.

For Jonas, part of her allure had been how she'd hold her head to the side, her ear in proximity to her right shoulder as if she were at a museum studying a complicated and dense painting from a particular angle. While walking or speaking with another person, she'd lower her head as if to avoid what she would see when she would look up and meet the doting gaze of her companion. Yet whenever she did make eye contact, she was surprisingly frank in her assessment, her gray-brown eyes sparkling with candor and at those times seemingly not shy at all. But her frankness was short-lived. For whenever the recipient of her candor returned it in kind she would immediately lower her gaze as if needing to hide what she had been intending to reveal. Jonas knew this well, as he was often that recipient. This led him to conclude that she hoped to scrutinize another's psyche, but did not want her own to be penetrated.

Not only was she evasive about her height, in her tendency to lower her head, but also about her slimness; she wore loose-fitting clothes, neutral colors, mostly pants and skirts with silky blouses.

Although he may have been the first man she had found compelling, there was nothing about her demeanor to suggest inexperience. She was composed—less romantic and more practical than her appearance indicated. And despite her shyness, which he naturally questioned, she was not naïve, nor was she cynical.

Because of her overprotective mother and strict father, both of whom had been born in Trieste of mixed ancestry—her mother, Austrian and Italian, and her father, Austrian and Flemish—Jonas soon realized Jenny carried with her European sensibilities and protocol. He noted how she had arranged it so that her friends interacted as little as possible with her parents, particularly with her mother. For if they were too much exposed to Mr. and Mrs. Smila, Jonas had gathered, Jenny believed it would brand her in the eyes of her peers as overly dutiful and perhaps passive. If her nature were different, Jonas supposed, she would have been a more rebellious eighteen-year-old. But rebellion was not her inclination. Instead she was tenacious, unlike anyone he had known.

Although he had come to know Jenny when she was eighteen, Jonas first had become aware of her four years earlier. Following his graduation from college he had returned home to learn that a new family had moved into the house next door. It was 1968 and he was twenty-three—because of his dreamy and skeptical nature, which at six had revealed itself as hesitancy, his mother had kept him home an extra year; she had decided he would not be mature enough to start school for another year.

Their neighborhood consisted of a row of ranch-style homes with back lawns that more often than not were overgrown. His mother had informed him about the Smilas the morning after his return. Her words were soft and persistent; she didn't want to discuss the alternative, which was his future. He had been an art major, and had no job prospects in sight. She feared he would be drafted and sent to Vietnam.

It was a hazy morning and over breakfast his mother spoke in a detailed and respectful way about the new family in the house next door, the Smilas. Jonas assumed this was the same manner she would use with her customers in her position as bank manager, a role she had worked diligently to achieve.

Jonas would later recall the shadow his mother created as she pressed her finger against the yellow-and-white checked tablecloth.

Soon the sun broke through the mist, and a breeze flowed in through the open window, lifting the half-drawn shade. The soft light illuminated the coffeepot on the stove, the percolator at the top of it now still, and the side of the refrigerator, a dark gold color. Soon he heard the shade slap gently back against the windowpane.

"Jonas," she said, giving him a quick and endearing smile. He believed she had named him Jonas because she'd come across the name in one of the novels she read. His mother had a predilection for westerns—reading or watching them on television or at the movies, her glasses on and a solemn expression crossing her face, as if soon afterward she intended to write an analytical essay.

"Jonas," she said again, her smile more abrupt. "The Smilas are Europeans, from Trieste, though their daughter, Jenny, an only child like yourself, was born here." It gave her an added confidence, he thought, that the Smilas presumably were interested in staying in America, which was important to her as a daughter of immigrants. "I spoke to Mrs. Smila—Johanna is her first name. She is an experienced and knowledgeable woman," Cora said, pressing her finger again on the table for emphasis. Jonas studied her deep brown eyes. There was something in her expression, particularly in her gaze, he had not before noticed—both steady and questioning, her lashes blinking more than usual, her mouth slightly open when she paused in her words, and he wondered what she really thought of Johanna Smila. He wasn't certain if in truth she loathed her, as he knew his mother would never acknowledge not liking anyone, or whether it was because Johanna Smila had piqued his mother's curiosity as very few people had done before.

After speaking with his mother, Jonas stepped out into the backyard. The sun shone brightly; it was unseasonably warm for a late spring day. He noted that his mother had recently had the lawn mowed. He went over to the lounge chair that she had parked in the middle of their small yard to sun herself.

He lay back in the chair and closed his eyes. It was difficult to fathom that he would not be returning to college. Memories from his days at school crossed his mind like a series of colorful fireworks on a sultry summer night—sparkly and fleeting. Then he thought about his conversation with his mother. He knew how worried she was about him, and he could not blame her. He realized her talking to him about the new neighbors had been her attempt at diverting herself from her concerns; it pained him that she worried about his future. Still, he gathered, to a certain extent she was impressed with Johanna Smila.

He opened his eyes and slowly looked to the side, glimpsing a young woman in the adjacent yard. He surmised she was Jenny Smila. His mother had mentioned that she was fourteen, but she looked younger. On a ledge close to the sloping roof of the garage she sat alone in a pool of shade. Her naturally curly hair was in a long, loose braid, her cheekbones high and defined, half-catching the light. In her hand was a tennis ball, which from time to time she'd bounce with surprising force and gusto against a dry patch of earth. While her throwing motion was awkward, her expression was surprisingly placid, reminding him of the young woman in Botticelli's *Primavera*. His thoughts turned to his junior year spent in Italy and France, traipsing through museums, drinking lots of wine, and his affair with an insouciant French woman named Claudine who sold postcards of the paintings at the Louvre. When he came out of his reverie, he looked over again at Jenny and saw she continued to pound the ball against the ground as if in doing so she was willing grass to grow. He was reluctantly intrigued.

Two weeks later, he received a call from a college friend who had moved to San Francisco about a possible job in an art gallery. His mother, who had always encouraged his interest in art, was elated to hear about the possibility of his working in a gallery. She paid for his plane ticket; two days later he boarded a flight to the West Coast.

Two

Summer

Outside her bedroom window the sky was gray with faint shafts of light falling tepidly over the sill. Jenny Smila closed her eyes and imagined the sun rising beyond the mist.

It was early April of 1972, her eighteenth birthday. How alone she was, she thought, grasping the blanket and pulling it close to her neck. She lifted her head and between the opening in the drapes she peered out at the still naked trees, the branches shaking from a sudden, brief wind.

Although she was born in Hartford, Connecticut, her parents were Europeans, who she felt were dismissive about her birthright. Their indifference to her American nature heightened her sense of alienation, more so than her not having a brother or sister. For no matter how often she'd visit the birthplace of her mother and father, she was keenly aware she was not from or of Trieste. Her disassociation from this city was not a choice she had made, but her reality. But she was not disheartened. To the contrary, she was filled with a subdued yet fluttering anticipation about her future, knowing she was strong. She was hopeful. And soon, she would be free.

Rapid knocks, a succession of them, on her bedroom door, before it creaked open. Within seconds her mother, cheeks flushed, appeared on the threshold, holding a tray; on it were two cups in her favorite china pattern, royal blue flowers on a white background, along with shiny silverware. As Jenny watched her mother approach she noticed Johanna's steps were hesitant at first, then swift, the cups and spoons rattling.

Johanna sat on the edge of the bed and placed the tray between them. Her mauve-colored silk robe revealed her ample cleavage and deepened her complexion and oval-shaped green eyes. She smiled and leaned forward as if about to relay a secret. Her voice sounding hoarse, she said she was not certain what the weather would be like that day; New England weather was unpredictable. She drank her coffee black and, after a few sips, added in her practical voice, gesticulating with her soft, round hand, that in one way or another it would be a beautiful day because it was Jenny's birthday. Jenny thought her mother appeared only mildly effervescent, her eyelids puffy; she gathered Johanna had not slept well. For her movements were muted, less spontaneous than usual, her gaze more fleeting. Jenny understood it was because she, her only child, was eighteen, an adult, and because of it Johanna felt older. Though deeply fond of her mother, Jenny knew she did not love her enough.

Between sips of coffee, Johanna chatted about what they would do that day. Jenny listened with guarded interest, considering how it must feel to be a mother of an eighteen-year-old, the mother of an only child. But she did not ponder this for long—she was not in her mother's position and might never be; she fully intended to have more than one child or no children at all. She had planned her future as far ahead as she could see. On some days her view was clear and expansive and on others quite cloudy. But clouds had never hampered her. She smiled at her mother and, knowing her as Jenny did, she believed Johanna sensed her daughter's concern. Her mother was reassured, her enthusiasm no longer dampened by fears of time passing too quickly. Johanna again was living in the present. Suddenly she placed her cup down on the tray and brought one hand to the side of her face. She hoped she had not burnt the toast, she announced. As Jenny watched, Johanna hastily left the room, neglecting to close the bedroom door. Jenny looked past the tray and empty cups, and out the window; the clouds had dispersed. Light flowed in through the opening in the apricot-colored drapes, and she felt a mingling of concern and hope.

After school that day, Jenny and her mother drove into Boston. Their destination was Maurice's shop on Newbury Street, where Jenny would be instructed to choose any outfit she liked, no matter the expense. It was much cooler now. Johanna turned up the heat in the car. Although her mother's movements in general were expansive and unrestricted, when she drove, Jenny noticed how Johanna would push herself forward in the seat and clutch the steering wheel with both hands, as if, no matter the weather or traffic, she was driving though a dense fog, surrounded by a myriad of cars.

Maurice's was their favorite clothing store in Boston; they had shopped there ever since they had moved from Hartford. Here they would go twice a year—on Jenny's birthday and, in early November, on Johanna's.

A bell tingled as they stepped inside the shop; they were promptly greeted by Maurice, the owner, a middle-aged man of average height with a crown of thick dark hair, muted by a slight graying around his temples.

"Good day, Madame, Mademoiselle. I have not seen you in a few months, yes?" he said impatiently. He motioned with his hand to a spiral staircase. Although Johanna wore high heels, she lithely climbed the steps, not holding on to the bannister. With a forced elegance, she turned her head to acknowledge Maurice, who trailed behind her. It was Jenny's eighteenth birthday, she said, and she hoped to see her in something more adult, no longer the loose-fitting clothes Jenny insisted on wearing. She was a woman now.

"Madame, your daughter has been a woman for a few years," he answered curtly. Jenny's throat tightened; she felt at first constricted by Maurice's words, then intrigued.

At the top of the stairway they stepped onto a plush white rug, which always surprised Jenny; it extended to the circular area on the right where there was a semicircle of full-length mirrors. Opposite the mirrors was a beige leather sofa and next to it a wide matching armchair. Between the sofa and the armchair was an antique wooden table; on it stood a vase of fresh white lilies.

Maurice disappeared, and Jenny and her mother sat on the sofa. Johanna rested one arm across the curved top and crossed her legs, her pocketbook at her feet. Smiling at her daughter, she drummed her fingers over the arm rest.

Maurice returned with an armful of dresses nearly covering his face. In an efficient manner, he instructed Jenny to stand in the center of the room, before the mirrors. She felt her flat shoes pressing into the soft, rich carpeting. When she caught her image, she noticed her expreccion was staitled. She had been thinking of their small, untidy home, the chipped linoleum on the kitchen floor and worn carpeting in the dining room, believing her parents should be spending their money on more practical items. She had been told by her mother that they bought her an expensive outfit once a year because they wanted her to be confident, but more often, she was embarrassed by their largesse.

Most of the dresses Maurice held up were straight and form-fitting. It was his practice to first show a dress to her mother, and then he'd turn to Jenny. Johanna would intently eye each one he presented, making comments such as not the right color for Jenny, not the right style, it would make her look too thin. Jenny would nod in response to each of her comments, hoping for a dress that was similar to her preferred style.

When she tried each one on, Jenny was surprised at how much she relished the feel of the material clinging to her body and experienced an unexpected sense of well-being.

Maurice had given her mother a little bell to summon him when she had changed and they were ready for his next appraisal. He was always quick and eager to point out how well a dress looked on Jenny or if it didn't suit her at all.

As they dined that night at a restaurant on Beacon Hill, Jenny studied her parents beneath the light of the chandelier; she was filled with a high regard for them as well as a slight suspicion. Her father was dressed in his finest suit, black with tiny gray lines. She thought her mother looked unnervingly beautiful in a kelly green dress with a low-cut neckline. Her auburn hair was swept up off her face, highlighting her high cheekbones and exotic green eyes. She wore a gold necklace with a square flat emerald stone. Johanna's mother had given it to her on her eighteenth birthday—Trieste, 1942, the war, Jenny thought—no matter how diligently she tried, she could not imagine her mother as an eighteen-year-old, and neither could she fathom how it was to live in the midst of a world war at that age. To her it was as if the war had occurred in another century, in another universe. For her parents never spoke of those years.

Jenny wore the dress her mother had purchased at Maurice's shop that afternoon. It was silk, sleeveless, black and white, low cut in the front, even lower cut in the back, and fitted to her form. Her hair had been especially curly that day so she had arranged it in a French braid wrapped around her head.

Her mother leaned forward and patted Jenny's hand, telling her she looked very beautiful. She didn't speak in a whisper, but in a tone loud enough for anyone nearby to hear. Jenny was disconcerted; what was most on her mind was the homework she had not finished that was due tomorrow. As if reading her thoughts, Johanna told her not to worry about her schoolwork, that she must enjoy her birthday—it comes only once a year. Jenny thought of their small home with the broken garage door and how once the spring progressed the grass in the backyard would be overgrown until her father was in the frame of mind to mow it. But she admitted to herself how much she was drawn to the luxury of the restaurant, the gold-framed mirrors, the glittering chandelier in the foyer and the smaller replicas scattered about the dining room. Yet again it struck her that they should not be there. This was not their reality; it would have been better for her to be home studying. But when she saw the delight written across the faces of her parents, she knew she must respect that this was what they desired.

Her father raised his wine glass and made a toast in her honor, saying that she had never appeared more elegant, that in less than six months' time she would be in college, away from them, that she was an adult now, that he respected her academic success. She lowered her eyes, overcome by his graciousness and his confidence in her. He had never been one to exaggerate or compliment her gratuitously. She wanted this moment to last forever. She did not know how to express her appreciation. Slowly she raised her eyes and gazed directly at him. "Thank you, Father," she said, and looked over at her mother, thanking her as well.

"Jenny, do not be so humble and demure, my darling. You do not need to thank us—don't you see, this is our way of thanking you for your poise, intelligence, and beauty," her mother said, gesticulating with one hand, the other touching her napkin at one moment, holding on to the side of her glass at the next. Johanna motioned for the waiter to pour more wine into their glasses. Jenny noticed a drop of moisture above her mother's lips. She was anxious, Jenny surmised, and her heart beat more quickly. She looked over at her father; he was smiling.

"Is something wrong, Jenny?" he asked. There was an uncharacteristic twinkle in his eyes. He was usually firm and serious, underscored by his narrow and erect frame. She saw he had put on the gold cuff links his father had given to him. There was a story she was not quite certain of regarding her grandfather hiding from the Germans during the war and those cuff links. Since neither of her parents spoke of the war, she had heard this story referred to in passing by a friend of her father's when they had been visiting Trieste a few summers before. His wearing the cuff links that night startled Jenny. She was beginning to believe there was something more to this evening, something she was not aware of. She felt a chill run up and down her bare arms.

"Are you cold, darling?" She felt her mother's moist hand over hers. Although Johanna's gaze was direct, Jenny noted her unease, perhaps even a trace of duplicity in her bearing. And she recalled her mother not telling her five or six years before that her great-grandmother had died. One day Jenny had come home from school and had found her mother in tears. Her heart pounding, she had asked her why she was sad, and her mother had looked at her in the same elusive way as she had now. What was she hiding this evening? Why was her father elated? She longed for his usual subdued self. She thought again of her great-grandmother, Nina— Jenny had not learned of her death until a year later; the information had come from her father as they were planning their next trip to Europe. He thought Johanna had told her by then. Were there other times when her mother had been evasive? She now wondered if she did not know the truth about a myriad of things. Different circumstances crossed her mind. She looked over at her mother, who was checking her watch.

The waiter came over to pour more wine into their glasses. Jenny felt dizzy. Although she had not had much to eat, she had been easily drinking the delicate wine.

When her mother looked up from her watch, alarm crossed her face. She met her husband's gaze. He shrugged. He was enjoying his meal and soon asked for the dessert menu. Johanna frowned and said, "It is nearly ten o'clock. Jenny has school tomorrow. She needs her rest. And you have to open the store early. You need your rest too."

Again, her father shrugged—his nonchalance was atypical, blurring the image Jenny carried of him as a once exacting engineer who had immigrated to the United States to work as a shoe salesman.

When they left the restaurant and ventured out into the Boston night, Jenny understood for varying reasons that the three of them were unsettled.

Over the two months that followed, Jenny noticed her mother becoming more and more restive. Johanna would often go next door to speak with Mrs. Hoffman, a widow, whose only son—Jonas—worked in an art gallery in San Francisco. He had not been home in four

years. Jenny was told that Mrs. Hoffman had gone out
to San Francisco on several occasions to visit him; sometimes she was accompanied by one or both of her two
sisters. Jenny believed she might have seen Jonas once.
Soon after their move from Hartford, Jenny had noticed
a man reclining in the lounge chair in Mrs. Hoffman's
backyard. But at best it was a hazy memory. She liked
to look at the photos of him that Mrs. Hoffman had
hung on her sitting room wall. The picture that endeared
him most to her was the photo of Jonas at sixteen, lying
languidly in the grass, his arms crossing his face, as if
shading himself from the rays of the sun, a scattering of
wild daisies surrounding him.

Whenever they visited Mrs. Hoffman, Johanna
would talk of Trieste society, as well as how diligently
she'd trained to become an opera singer. While her
mother spoke, Jenny would focus on Mrs. Hoffman, her
rapt expression, the energy she exuded, her overall posture of optimism, and how Mrs. Hoffman's questioning
and sensitive eyes closely watched her mother.

Because of Mrs. Hoffman's presence in their life,
for Jenny, the name Hoffman had become synonymous
with America—spirited, forward-looking—in a way
Smila never would. For she would forever align the
name Smila with their days in Hartford, where Jenny
as a child would observe other adults, visitors she did

not know, in their living room, many smoking heavily, speaking a foreign language, their expressions fraught with angst and a wary hope.

On an afternoon in late June, Jenny went out to the chaise longue. From her seat, she watched the sun slip behind the clouds. In her hands was Roth's *Goodbye, Columbus*. Most of her friends had read it when the movie version had come out a few years earlier. Her mother had insisted Jenny wait to read it at least until she graduated from high school. Johanna herself had not read the book, and had announced unequivocally she would never do so; she preferred European authors. "American authors favor action; European authors write deep, complex novels, novels that touch the soul. You are an American," she admonished her daughter. "Naturally you are inclined to read American books."

Jenny now lowered her head and read with abandon, her eyes running across the page. Drawn into the novel, she was not aware of how much time had passed. Slowly she heard voices, a conversation in the next yard. There was a slight breeze; the words floated in her direction. She did not look up from her book. She recognized the quick and round tone of Mrs. Hoffman's voice. Her words were low, but clear. She soon gathered that Jonas would be home on the first of July, and that he'd be spending the summer at a gallery on Newbury Street that was affiliated with the one in San Francisco where he'd been working.

"Cora, the truth is you don't want Jonas to meet Harold—I don't understand why you are so squeamish about their meeting."

Mrs. Hoffman answered, "I think it is because he never knew his father and I can only imagine what illusions he must harbor about him—probably even he doesn't realize how much he idolizes David."

"You were terribly in love with David," Belinda responded earnestly.

Mrs. Hoffman was silent for a few minutes. "This is about Jonas, Belinda," Mrs. Hoffman answered abruptly. "I can't think of the past—it isn't good, it isn't helpful."

"Jonas is an adult, twenty-seven; he will not be surprised about Harold, and he won't become preoccupied with thoughts of David's absence in his life. You have protected him, Cora. You are not respecting him, his maturity."

Mrs. Hoffman's voice now was so low, Jenny could no longer hear her. She might have become suddenly aware of Jenny's presence. She didn't look up from her book and imagined Mrs. Hoffman motioning to her companion that she was in the next yard. Jenny heard a screen door squeak open, and then shut. She looked up from her book; they had gone inside.

That evening after dinner, Jenny accompanied her mother to Mrs. Hoffman's house. As they walked through the front door, Jenny recalled she hadn't been there in more than a year. The foyer looked smaller, the furniture in the sitting room more crowded together than she remembered. There was a pleasant aroma of lilacs from a thick burning candle on top of the television set.

Johanna leaned forward in her seat, resting her hand on her daughter's knee, and said, "Jenny needs to find a more sophisticated and intellectual group of friends now that she will be going to college."

Mrs. Hoffman nodded in agreement. "You never know what anyone truly believes, where anyone really stands nowadays." Jenny and her mother glanced at each other, not knowing what Mrs. Hoffman meant. Jenny soon understood she was referring to the war in Vietnam. Mrs. Hoffman, her cheeks slightly reddening, rose reflexively from her chair and went into the kitchen to make coffee.

When she returned and handed them each a cup, the muted evening light caressing her form, she told them her son Jonas would be home for the summer, working in an art gallery on Newbury Street. Jenny studied Mrs. Hoffman, her short brown hair, her longish neck, her heart-shaped lips, and it dawned on Jenny that she was not simply a middle-aged, long-suffering widow who worked in a bank. Her respect for her grew. Next to Mrs. Hoffman her mother did not seem as approachable or real.

According to her mother, Mrs. Hoffman's son had been home for ten days, but Jenny had not yet caught a glimpse of him. He had become somewhat of an enigma for her; she was more and more uncertain whether or not the man she had seen in the lounge chair four years earlier had been Jonas. Lately she had been having dreams of a man in a black cape, whose face was shaded by a low-brimmed hat. *Jonas?* she'd ask, tugging at the cape in her dream. But when she tugged too hard he fell facedown and shattered as if all along he had been a glass statue.

During the day her mother would often urge her to walk to the beach, which was about a mile and a half from their home. Jenny noticed her father appeared more distracted than usual—he'd leave early every morning and then come home from the shoe store without saying very much. He would become absorbed in reading the newspaper or watching a baseball game on a small black-and-white television set, his foot tapping the floor, a thin burning cigar in the ashtray on the table next to him.

From time to time it struck Jenny that her parents might consider returning to Trieste. She could see the disaffection in their expressions, the sense of loss they wore so easily. She knew some of their close friends had gone back.

Toward the end of the second week of July, Jenny decided to take her mother's advice and walk to the beach. It was not too warm; a slight breeze caressed her arms. When she turned to look back at her home she saw that her mother was at the window and instead of drawing away so that Jenny might not catch her watching, Johanna waved in an encouraging way as if prodding her forward. Jenny smiled half-heartedly, though she did hasten her step. After walking far enough so that her mother could no longer see her, Jenny slowed down again. But soon she was crossing the busy main street.

The beach was crowded. She went to the spot across from a restaurant where she and her parents went whenever they came to the beach. She looked for a space to sit on the low cement wall that bordered the sand and the sidewalk; the ocean was about fifty yards away. It was soothing to watch the waves come in and break at the water's edge. People were sprawled out on towels or in lounge chairs across the sand, and some children carried plastic buckets filled with either water or sand.

She wore her bathing suit beneath her clothes. After she had found an empty spot on the wall, she removed her sleeveless blouse and sat in her shorts and the top of her two-piece bathing suit. Soon she lay down, using her blouse as a pillow. Her knees raised, she closed her eyes and listened to the crashing waves and the cawing seagulls. As she inhaled the smell of the ocean, a fine wind fingered her hair. After a while, she opened her eyes and noticed a shadow at her feet. When she looked up, she saw a man in shorts and a T-shirt sitting close to her, his long legs dangling, his toes hidden in the sand. She half raised herself, her elbows supporting her, scraping against the concrete. He looked over, his eyes steely and determined. He had blond-brown hair with slight curls that made him appear as if he were wearing a wreath on his head. He caught her gaze, and waved as if saluting her, then quickly, easily, he said her name.

His name was Eric Stram. He was thirty-eight years old. His body was long and narrow, his laugh, short and sharp. Jenny gathered that her mother had telephoned him to say she'd be at the beach that day and where to find her. He told her that Johanna, a friend of his parents, had sent him a photo of her about six months before.

She was flattered by his attention, his interest. He was not unattractive, yet she did not want to rush her life along. Like her parents, Eric was from Trieste. He was born in 1934; Johanna had been ten years old.

When her mother came into her room the next morning with a coffee mug in hand, Jenny sat up in bed. Taking the cup from her mother, she bluntly announced that Eric was much too old for her, that she did not want to rush her life along.

"His parents helped my family," Johanna responded, stopping herself from saying more. Then she said sharply, "Don't tell me about rushing your life along, you were not in Europe in the thirties and forties—we did not have a choice but to rush our lives along." She walked over to Jenny's bedroom window and, with one swift motion, pushed aside the drapes. Jenny drank more coffee from the mug. Her mother turned and said, "Jenny, you don't know what it is to struggle."

When Jenny met her gaze, Johanna looked away. Jenny wondered what she was not telling her. With guarded respect she answered, "I understand, Mother, but your struggles belong to the past; the past is not the present."

"Don't be naïve, Jenny," Johanna said caustically. As her mother moved toward the door, Jenny said curtly that she would let Eric know she would go to dinner with him the next evening. In her mother's uplifted chin and pursed lips, Jenny read how conflicted she was.

It was too warm to walk to the beach. Jenny took her book—she was now reading Lawrence's *Women in Love*—and went to the chaise longue in the backyard. She began to read but became drowsy from the sun; her eyes soon closed. She did not know how much time had passed when she heard someone call out her name. She opened her eyes and realized it was Jonas, recognizing him from the photos she had seen on the walls in Mrs. Hoffman's home. He stood at the low gate that separated the Smilas' yard from the Hoffmans'. She sat up and removed her sunglasses. With one hand she shaded her eyes from the sun.

"That is, I assume you are Jenny," he said. He was older than she was but not as old as Eric. His mannerisms were more like someone of her age. His tone, slightly comedic, enticed her. He told her he had the day off, that he was Jonas, Mrs. Hoffman's son. "She's told me about you," he said. Jenny had not yet spoken. She continued to study his face, which looked more scrunched up because of his mustache, and lightly cynical, yet his body had a looseness about it that defied his skepticism. In a way, she had known him—or, more accurately, known of him—for four years. Without a second thought, she

39

got up and went over to him; her feet were bare and the hot tar near the gate stung them. Her bathing suit was slightly dislodged. He held a sketch pad in his hand. They shook hands, and she avoided his penetrating gaze. He was an inch taller than she was. She asked him if he was an artist. "More of a dilettante," he said and smiled.

She asked to see what he was sketching. He held the pad on top of the gate, and she saw that he had been drawing the back of his home, and then off to the side she noticed he had added her in the chaise longue. It was only a small part of his sketch. She smiled. "Very nice," she said.

He shrugged. "Hope you don't mind I have included you. If you like, I could take you out."

"It's okay," she answered. Then he put the pad down on the grass. They talked for a while about his work in the art gallery, and that she did not have a job. He asked her if she'd like to go to a movie that night—as friends, as neighbors. It's not a date, he assured her. She told him that she was already going with her friends— would he like to come along? She was caught off guard when he said yes. A breeze crossed through their yards. Before she knew it, she was back in the chair and he had disappeared inside his home. She could not determine whether or not she was pleased about his coming that night.

~

The next day Jenny thought her mother was apprehensive about her date with Eric that evening. Johanna paced in front of the dining room table, her cheeks flushed. Afternoon light streamed through the dining room window. Johanna stopped pacing and crossed her arms, her sturdy wrists illuminated by the sun. She sighed, then recommended Jenny wear the dress she and her father had bought for her eighteenth birthday. Then her mother rested her hands on the table and lowered her head. "Be kind to him," she said in a low, intense voice.

A few hours later, after she had showered, she heard a knock on her bedroom door. Her mother rushed in. Her expression forlorn, she told Jenny that Eric had called to cancel dinner because of an important and unexpected business meeting. Jenny was both relieved and annoyed.

She carried a heavy black suitcase to her father's car. The trunk was open; she put the luggage inside, then slammed shut the lid, her forehead damp from the heat. She would be leaving for college the next day. Jenny did not wonder what lay ahead of her, but instead her thoughts turned to the past few months. She realized it would have been a more fruitful summer if she had had a job and had been able to spend more time with people closer to her age. Not having had a job had distanced her more than she liked from her high school friends, and now that August was nearly over she felt a sense of loss for what could have been.

The previous night she had said good-bye to Jonas. He would flying back to San Francisco that day; he may now be on the plane, she thought. He had been a good friend that summer. He had listened to what she had had to say about Eric, and her mother's insistence that she be kind to him. He seemed to acknowledge and agree, though with an unmistakable hesitancy, that Eric—the worldly Eric, they called him—was too old for her. He said he found it interesting that she had kept her friends from knowing her parents and she smiled, but didn't add anything to his comment.

As it turned out, Eric had been quite busy with his work that summer. She had had dinner with him only twice. Neither time had he touched her, other than to shake her hand. They conversed as if they were brother and sister. Her mother sensed that nothing of significance had happened between them, and Jenny was aware of Johanna's disappointment.

Her favorite part of the summer had been going down to Jonas's basement, where he had set up an art studio. She found his paintings hazy, not fully developed, but that is what she most liked about them, about him—he had so much more to go; observing his confidence rising as he cautiously improved had elated her.

The previous night she and Jonas had walked to the beach. Sitting on the concrete wall, their legs dangling, they had watched the waves lapping the shore. Steeling herself, her heart pounding, she asked him if he was planning to kiss her good-bye. "I will do so only if you ask with a smile; you look so serious, Jenny," he answered. They laughed and then kissed, and although it was not a very long kiss it was much more intense than she had expected.

Without speaking, they slowly walked in the direction of their street. The night was warm and the light from the moon reflected over the sidewalk before them, their shadows in stark contrast. When they arrived at her home, Jonas walked with her to the front door and said, his voice low, his expression doubtful, "Friends, we are just friends, Jenny." Closely she watched as he backed away from her. As he climbed the front steps of his house, his form was more and more illuminated by the light shining from the front porch. Suddenly he stopped and waved to her. By the time she raised her hand, he had disappeared inside his home.

Three

San Francisco

There had been a light rain that morning, splashing the hydrangeas Cora had planted months before, but by the time they left for the airport it was mid-afternoon, and it had turned into a steamy and still late August day. The roads now dry, they drove in near silence, mostly music from the now-disbanded Beatles playing on the car radio, interspersed from time to time with news flashes. Jonas, reflecting on the past summer, tuned out the latest world events. And because of her quietude, the way she loosely guided the steering wheel with one hand, her elbow resting where the window had been rolled down, her lips closed, he supposed Cora was doing the same.

Silently he acknowledged that the tension between them the past two months had been a result of their inability to reveal to each other who they had become. It struck him how eager he was to be free of her presence, not because he didn't love her, but because she was an incessant reminder to him of his fatherless existence.

After embracing, and as Jonas was about to board the plane, he turned to look back at her. Meeting his gaze, Cora lifted her hand and waved with assurance. It was her attempt to convey her support of him, her trust that he would go forward with his life as best he could, but most importantly without any hindrance from her. Again he turned away, but immediately he stole one last look, a quick glance she did not notice. Her arms were folded, her eyes steady and attentive, her chin lifted as if she were bracing herself for her life without him at home. Surely she would be able to meet more often with Harold, Jonas sharply thought—Harold, whom he had not met and whose existence his mother had refused to acknowledge. And so his leaving was as much a gain for her as it would be a loss.

As he walked down the aisle to his seat, he thought about how he had longed to ask if she perceived his father in him at all. One evening in mid-July they had dined out together; she had taken the day off from work, and her mood was more mellow than usual. She had looked up from the menu she was holding, smiling, and had begun to ask what he wanted to eat but stopped suddenly, her eyes startled, and said, "The expression on your face, Jonas, you remind me of someone, how serious you seem, but I can't recall who it is." She shrugged and then peered down again at the menu. Yet as she grasped it, he saw her hand shake for a moment and he knew she was thinking of David, his father. There were other times—he could not recall the exact details of where they were or what they had been doing—all he remembered was he was unable to ask the question he most needed an answer to. He knew it was because he did not possess the courage to ask. His heart would pound fiercely whenever he considered doing so.

In the past she had mentioned his father in broad terms; she'd say, her voice soft, precise, "Your father liked to go to the movies—you know I like westerns, but he preferred Hitchcock," or she'd tell Jonas that David's favorite sport had been basketball. Or that he was tall, and serious, but sometimes when she least expected it he'd tell her a very funny joke. She'd speak of David's personality in general, never allowing Jonas to learn who his father was: what he had hoped for, what he had most feared, what he had been most passionate about.

He acknowledged that what had prevented him from asking more about his father was that he had become senselessly preoccupied with what he had found more pressing at the time—namely, her relationship with Harold.

As the pilot backed up the plane and prepared to taxi down the runway, Jonas looked out the small window, his eyes resting on his mother, who stood inside behind the expansive airport window, her face pressed against the glass. From that wavy distance her brown eyes in his mind appeared more sad than focused, her posture more relaxed than erect. It was a mood and bearing he had not witnessed in her that summer. Instead she had been mostly alert and forthright in her actions and words. He felt a twinge of guilt, wondering if despite her independent nature, and her relationship with the mysterious Harold, she might need her son to be close for reasons Jonas understood were beyond him.

They had not lived together for that long of a period in years. And so that summer there had been times when they'd been irritated with each other and those first annoyances had been the beginnings of a subtle but undeniable tension between them. He was aware of how much it bothered her when he went out with his friends from high school for the night and didn't call to let her know he wouldn't be home until the next day. But this provided him with a sense of independence—he no longer was simply her son, no longer guided by her sense of right and wrong—and so he had felt justified. For he had been severely disappointed that she had refused to tell him about Harold. If she had been frank about it, as she was about most things, he would have been supportive of the relationship and wished her well.

It had taken him nearly a month to realize she was involved in a serious relationship. Whenever she was about to leave, she'd tell him she would be going to a movie or shopping with her sisters. One evening when he'd been home for over three weeks, Belinda had called to speak with his mother, and he had answered promptly that she was at the movies. Hastily Belinda had said, "Ah, yes." Before he had had a chance to say more she had hung up the phone. He waited up for his mother. He sat alone with the lights off in front of the television. When she came in at midnight, he instinctively jumped up and asked where she had been. Yawning, she said sleepily that she had gone to a movie with her sisters.

"You weren't with Belinda. She called, asking for you," he said, speaking, he supposed, with the edginess of a suspicious husband.

Though weary, she studied him for a moment, her gaze impassive, and said flatly, "I was with Rina." Closely he watched as she turned away, her compact and defiant form moving toward her bedroom door; she opened it, then disappeared inside. Soon he heard the click of the lock. He stood there, faintly reassured. He believed her; he had not ever known her to lie to him.

A week later, a Friday morning, before they each left for work, he told her he'd be spending the night in Boston with friends from San Francisco who were visiting for the weekend. She nodded, but there was no change in her expression. When he got to the gallery, one of his friends called from Chicago to say that the three of them would come the following weekend instead; they wanted to spend more time there, go to a Cubs game. He had not driven the car he was renting for the summer to work that day because it would have been costly and difficult to find overnight parking.

He took the subway home. When he walked into the house, his mother was not there. After he made himself a quick peanut butter sandwich, he went to the basement to work on a painting he'd begun the previous weekend. An hour or two later, he heard the front door open and shut. Then he heard his mother's voice, followed by a distinctly masculine one Jonas did not recognize. He was stunned; his heart beat more quickly. The muted interplay of their voices suggested a deep intimacy. He guessed his mother had been so preoccupied with him that she had not noticed the light on in the basement when they had come up the front walkway. Soon he heard their footsteps in the kitchen, their voices closer and more clear than they'd been at first. Jonas stood in the middle of the basement, a brush in his raised hand; it was a stifling night and he felt moisture from the heat running down his face. He was torn between his desire to hear their words, yet hoping not to. "You never acknowledge you love me or care for me. Why should I introduce you to my son?" His heart skipped a beat at his mother's sharp tone. "You are disillusioned about love, Harold, that is your problem."

"And you aren't?"

"No, I loved my husband, but I lost him long ago. I try to remember David, but it is difficult. My memories of him are not lasting. He has become more like a character I have read about in a book. Sometimes I think he never existed."

Then there was silence. Jonas imagined his mother bowing her head and covering her face with her hands. And he soon heard them walk out of the kitchen and down the hallway. He had only heard Harold speak those three words—his voice tired, as if he had had a few glasses of beer.

Jonas spent an uncomfortable and sleepless night on a dusty old sofa. Defiant and angry, he forced himself not to consider what might be happening above.

At six o'clock the next morning, a Saturday, he tiptoed up the stairs and left the house through the kitchen door. Hastily he walked the three blocks to the main street. It was a drizzly and misty morning, the temperature had dropped some, and he was relieved that the coffee shop was open. To help pass the time he had brought a small sketch pad with him and a piece of charcoal. Between gulps of coffee he attempted to draw the likeness of the waitress behind the counter as well as any customers who came into the shop. But his sketches were more like caricatures and eventually, out of frustration, he placed the pad facedown on the table and ordered another cup of coffee. When he swiveled round on his seat he noticed at the takeout counter a slim man of average height with dark hair combed to the side, in his forties. Maybe it was his imagination, but he thought it was the same tired male voice of the night before, and he wondered if it was Harold. He picked up his sketch pad and started to draw him but, deeply conflicted, he soon gave up. Yet whenever he pondered Harold and his mother's relationship, an image of this man would come to mind.

A week later he attempted to bring up the subject of Harold. It was a sunny Sunday morning, and he and his mother were sitting on the back porch drinking coffee and savoring the beginning of what would be a warm summer day. His mother pointed out the hydrangeas, blooming a periwinkle blue color. Then she turned to him, sunlight heightening the thoughtful expression in her eyes, and she asked, studiously, about his work at the gallery. Jonas knew she relished hearing him describe the customers who came into the gallery, how they would decide on what to buy and how he would help them choose a painting. On this day she was inquiring about a particular client she had seen at the gallery when she had visited Jonas in San Francisco a few years before. She had noticed him when she had come in one day to take Jonas out to lunch. The customer had mainly liked to collect lithographs. She remembered him because she thought he'd looked overly tired, but had not allowed his weariness to hamper his interest in the works Jonas was showing him. Jonas told her that he had passed away a year before and his wife had remarried soon afterward. Then he turned to his mother and said nonchalantly that it would be nice if she could get married again, she was still relatively young. But she looked back at him in a stunned way. "Jonas, I don't want to marry again." Abruptly, she got up and opened the kitchen door to go inside.

Following her in, he said, "I hope you aren't saying this for my sake. I am hoping you will remarry. In fact, I want you to marry again." He sat across from her at the table; she was looking over the surface of it as if something was missing. And then she got up and took a pitcher of iced coffee out of the refrigerator.

Her back to him, she said, "The answer is still the same, Jonas. I don't want to marry again." When she sat down and poured the iced coffee into a tall glass, she gave him a brief and tired smile.

And so on that late August day as he studied his mother standing at the airport window, he regretted he had not had the chance to meet Harold. Grudgingly he understood she needed and deserved privacy.

Once he arrived in San Francisco Jonas was pleased to have returned to the Bay Area. In his apartment, he thrust open the windows to survey the city, but his view was limited; he caught sight of his neighbor's kitten staring at him from the opposite pane, her tiny paw on the glass.

After ten days or so he began to feel disoriented. Unexpected images of his mother, her expression set, as he tried to provoke her into admitting that one day she might want to marry again. And he'd often muse over one of the paintings he had been working on and had left in the basement. It was a painting of a seagull flying low above the waves. There was something lacking in it—a sense of the bird's strength, he thought. But Jenny had said it had potential. She had liked to linger in the basement and study his paintings. She seemed absorbed by his work, which had puzzled him, as his paintings were far from what he wanted them to be. "Jonas," she'd say, "I like that you don't flaunt color. You are reserved with color and I find it interesting—it is your style, your uniqueness." He told her it was because his paintings were at an early stage—he still had a long way to go. Most of his life he'd had an intense sense of color, and he silently wondered if working at the gallery had dampened it.

He soon realized how disgruntled he had become about his work in the gallery. While on Newbury Street, it had occurred to him that he might have lost his ability to sell. At first he had attributed it to the fact that it wasn't as robust of a market as the one in San Francisco. But after the first few months he wasn't selling as much in San Francisco as he had in the past. He was less enthusiastic when explaining the story behind a painting or a painter and how the work had landed in the gallery. In fact, he thought he sounded rather bland and almost discouraging. Jonas gradually realized it was because what he really wanted was not to sell art, but instead to sketch and paint.

While in Boston, he'd had only an inkling of a desire to establish himself as a painter. The only person he had discussed it with had been his aunt Rina, who worked not far from the gallery. She would meet him for lunch on Newbury Street, usually at a restaurant nearby specializing in crepes that she liked to go to. They'd often sit outside. She enjoyed telling him about her fiancé, Dan. He was from Connecticut and she had met him about a year before on the train to New York. He had boarded at Stamford; and she had been on the train coming in from Boston. She was now in her mid-forties. During one of their lunches, between inhalations of her cigarette, she said he was a year younger than she was and had never been married before because he had cared for his sister's family after her husband had died. "He has a big heart, like your father." And she had smiled in her warm way, her lips closed, her eyes penetrating his.

It had been difficult for Jonas to accept that Rina was engaged. From time to time she'd have a faraway look in her eyes, as she had had in the past, but at those times, he knew she was physically present. Now she was not as fully with him as before.

One extremely warm day in early August they had gone inside for lunch; it was too hot to sit out on the restaurant patio. Jonas lowered his voice and confided in her about his growing interest in becoming a painter. Mildly surprised, her eyes widening, Rina bowed her head and snuffed out her cigarette. He knew by the way she pressed her lips together, her brow furrowed, that she was deciding what she thought about it. When she had finished extinguishing the cigarette, she looked up at him, her eyes caring and elusive, and said in a hushed voice, "Yes, Jonas. For heaven's sake—let yourself go."

After lunch, he walked toward the gallery, and by the time he went inside Rina's words had slipped from his mind.

In addition to his mother having a lover and his aunt Rina's engagement, another surprise for him the summer he returned to the East Coast had been that his mother had developed a strong relationship with Jenny's mother, Johanna Smila. His mother had never had many friends; she had relied socially on her sisters and their network of acquaintances. But he should have realized his mother's interest had been piqued by Johanna when she had spoken of her with uncharacteristic intensity four years earlier. Yet during the summer of his return he had not seen much of Johanna—running into her a few times as she was leaving his home and as he was coming in or going out. Although they had become close, whenever his mother mentioned Johanna to him she did so with disbelief and frustration, usually because of what Johanna had revealed to her in their most recent conversation. They were only a few years apart in age, his mother had told him, and his guess was their friendship continued and to a certain degree grew because his mother connected with her on some obscure level. He knew in a practical sense his mother doubted for the most part whatever Johanna said about her past life, and that, like a persistent sheriff, Cora deduced that at some point the truth about Johanna would be revealed.

One day Jonas asked if she thought Jenny was similar to her mother—she had just described to him with a certain amount of frustration what Johanna had said about her childhood in Trieste, and how she could not quite piece together why Johanna's family had been given a sapphire bracelet by a foreign dignitary visiting the city. At that point Jonas had been to the movies and to the beach on the weekend with Jenny only a few times. It was shortly before he brought her to his art studio in the basement. His mother, who had resumed reading an article from one of the various magazines she'd neatly arranged on top of the coffee table, turned to him and paused to collect her thoughts, then said in an abstracted way, her mind obviously more compelled now by the article she had been reading, that Jenny was quiet and not at all like her mother—she holds things in more. You know how Johanna exaggerates. Jenny isn't inclined to make things better or worse than they are. She sees what she sees and that is that. And his mother bowed her head and continued to read the magazine. He wasn't certain if she had been talking more about herself than about Jenny. Nonetheless her words about Jenny intrigued him and so soon after that conversation he had invited Jenny to see his studio in the basement.

He had noticed that with her friends Jenny seemed like one of the crowd, one eighteen-year-old indistinguishable from the next eighteen-year-old. He felt like the protective older brother whenever they asked his advice or wanted to know his opinion about the war in Vietnam. He'd refrain from talking about the war; although it was a different war, he would conflate mention of any war with his father's passing.

In San Francisco, he easily re-established himself with his friends and cleaned up his apartment; it was small and on a narrow street. He bought a print of Monet's *Charing Cross Bridge* and a large mirror to open up the space. But his heart was not in his attempts to improve his apartment—he thought more and more of the studio he had set up in his mother's basement as well as the paintings he had not finished. He recalled Rina's words. Then he thought of Jenny in the studio. She had become part of the scene in his imagination; he had mentally sketched her in the background just as he had drawn her off to the side in the chaise longue the day they first spoke at the gate separating their backyards.

One breezy late October afternoon, Frank, the owner of the gallery, approached Jonas and said he'd like to take him out for a drink. The sky was a vibrant blue, and as they walked up Powell Street, Jenny's words about his reserved use of color crossed his mind. At that moment he promised himself he would paint the sky the very same vibrant blue when he returned home and completed the painting of the seagull. They went to a hotel bar located on the top floor. They ordered drinks, then looked out at the bay. Frank asked Jonas if there was something on his mind, if something was bothering him, some personal problem. "Ever since you returned from the East Coast, Jonas, you haven't been yourself, you seem less enthusiastic, less engaged, and others have noticed it as well," he said, looking away. Jonas shrugged, answering that nothing specifically was bothering him, but he agreed, he had lost his enthusiasm. Frank, turning to him, appeared surprised by Jonas's honesty. Looking out at the bay again, both of them were silent. Then Jonas said maybe it would be best if he resigned, maybe he was no longer very good at selling art, maybe he'd better try something else. He did like to paint, after all.

Jonas remained in San Francisco until the following May. He supported himself by working as a waiter and found a more affordable apartment where he set up a space in the alcove to paint. Still not pleased with his work, he would often think of Jenny's comment about his use of color. No matter how diligently he worked with color, he felt his paintings appeared more and more reticent. For he wasn't able to let himself go as Rina had encouraged.

He refrained from telling his mother he had left the gallery, waiting until the end of the year to do so. He sensed she was uneasy with his decision, yet she calmly asked what he wanted to do next. And when he told her he wanted to paint, she seemed to accept it, though she added that it might be better for him to do so closer to home—after all, he had set up a studio in the basement. He could work odd jobs just as easily in Boston and could save money by living at home. Wouldn't he then be able to spend more time developing his craft?

Jonas listened intently to her words, knowing she was and always would be both practical and accepting. He was never certain if she was this way because he was fatherless or because she was naturally flexible.

Another reason he stayed in San Francisco was because he had become involved in a relationship with a woman named Miranda. Older than he was, she was very much part of the anti-war protests. Although he liked to hear her thoughts about the war, he stayed away from the protests himself. The war reminded him too much of his father's short existence—his sense of conflict only having grown.

He had met Miranda at a bus stop six weeks before he left the gallery. Usually he had walked to work, but it was a little cooler that day and he had neglected to put on a jacket. They were the only two waiting for the bus. She wore sunglasses, but when she took them off, which she did from time to time, her expression was soft yet unflinching—reminding him of Klimt's *Portrait of Gertrud Loew*. When the bus finally came, they climbed on. There were only two adjoining seats available; they sat next to each other. Soon the bus was stuck in traffic, and Jonas regretted not having walked. He would be late, and that day he was responsible for opening the gallery. Out of anxiety and restlessness, he began to tap his foot. Miranda turned to him and said, her voice clear and fine, "Please stop." He did as she requested, but was annoyed. Then she again removed her sunglasses and smiled warmly at him. He saw there were little lines surrounding her eyes and he thought she might be about five years older than he was. They went out to dinner that night. She insisted on treating him and said he could pay the next time.

At dinner Miranda spoke in an intense and pointed way about the anti-war movement and her involvement with it over the past few years. He told her he respected her ideals. Then he explained about his father's death. She looked at him across the table, her eyes warm and muddy, and smiled just as she had in the bus; again she reminded him of the Klimt painting.

Their relationship lasted until the first of January. Although she ostensibly seemed to understand his resistance to protesting, and how it related to his memories of growing up without a father, ultimately she needed him to share the experience with her.

One day they met directly after she had returned from a march. The sign she carried said, "Love is so much more than war; for it creates life." She seemed more elated than usual, more invigorated. Her usual pale complexion was now a deep pink and her eyes were bright with anticipation. Over a candlelight dinner Jonas had assiduously prepared, she raised her wine glass and told him it disturbed her that he refused to take part in the protests. Her words pained him; they were a reminder to him of how much the past was restraining him.

After his experience with Miranda, he threw himself more and more into painting. His work as a waiter was an afterthought; he'd go from table to table in a state of dissociation. Painting had become his reality. After a few months, and as May was approaching, he called his mother to let her know he would leave San Francisco in the next few weeks.

He perceived that although she was excited about his coming home, she was concerned as well. "I'm interested in hearing your plans, how you will manage to become an artist, a very good one," she said, her tone subdued. He imagined she was mentally calculating how she would rearrange her time with her lover, but then he lightly added that he knew about her relationship with Harold. There was silence at the other end of the phone. And then she continued to talk as if he hadn't revealed anything. But he thought he'd heard her sigh. At the end of the conversation she said brightly, "We can each go on with our lives now."

She had not come out to visit him that spring, and before his call he had wondered if she had planned to put it off until early autumn. She had often mentioned during her trips to San Francisco that she imagined it would very beautiful in September or October. She had neglected to say why she would not be coming that spring—she had not said anything at all. It had been as if she had forgotten about her yearly trip. Knowing her and the way she lived an ordered life, it seemed out of character that she had not mentioned it to him. Maybe it was because she had sensed he would be coming home soon. Or she hadn't planned a trip because of Harold's schedule.

He wasn't certain how long he would stay in the Boston area—he had thoughts of moving to New York once he was more settled in with his work. All he knew was he had no intention of moving west again. California was where he had failed, he concluded.

Once home, he spent most of each day in the basement studio he had set up the previous summer. Because he had saved money while working at the gallery in San Francisco, and because the tips he'd earned as a waiter had been plentiful, he was able to contribute money to day-to-day expenses. He was pleased he was not a financial burden on his mother. If he went out, he went to museums to study works of other artists—all he wanted was to learn. He was so focused, he did not call his old friends. He thought only of painting.

At the museum he'd stand in front of a Matisse and try to imagine what the painter was thinking and seeing when he drew a particular line, used a specific color. He studied other artists as well, but Matisse was the one he was most drawn to.

His mother was not concerned that he did not have a steady job—he thought she was happy to see him every morning. He knew after a certain amount of time elapsed she would encourage him to go out into the world again and away from the cocoon of her basement. For now she was patient.

In late May—Jonas had been home for about three weeks—he ran into Jenny at the drugstore on the main street. She had just completed her first year of college and couldn't have been home for long because, despite his monk-like existence, he would surely have bumped into her sooner. She didn't seem overjoyed to see him. She was wearing glasses and her hair was pulled back in a ponytail. She had changed from her year away, he thought. She stood more erectly now, no more head to the side. "Hi, Jonas," she said quite coolly, though her eyes were warm. He was reassured that her feelings toward him had not changed. "Are you home for a visit?" she asked evenly. He realized that although he'd been home for a few weeks, his mother must not have told Johanna. As they walked together in the direction of their respective homes, he explained to her about his decision to become a painter and how he was hoping to go to New York in a year or so. He wanted to be part of the nucleus of the art world, he said and smiled.

She looked at him doubtfully and answered, "I am very happy to hear you are painting full time, Jonas, but New York is not far away. You could go there now if you really wanted to, once a month at the least." In saying this he knew she had discerned his hesitation, his doubts.

A scowl crossed his face; he answered defiantly, "I am not quite ready, Jenny." She smiled, seemingly pleased with his honesty.

She then told him about her first year of college, how she had been puzzled by certain things and not very surprised about others. She thought the atmosphere would have been more intellectual, more philosophical. But instead the discourse between students had been more pragmatic and it had taken her a while to conform. It was clear as she spoke, he thought, that she had already made the adjustment. He imagined her sitting in various coffee shops with her classmates, especially on cold Saturday afternoons, sipping coffee or hot chocolate, dressed in a heavy sweater, hoping to have a discussion about something they'd read in class, trying to break in and mention a novel or essay they had recently studied.

But instead her classmates had preferred to talk about the practical side of their relationships with their boyfriends, or possible approaches to a profitable career.

Jenny didn't mention anything about the worldly Eric, nor did she mention a new boyfriend, and so he didn't pursue it.

The previous summer his mother had warned him not to get too close to Jenny—she was too young for him, and Eric, although he was older, might be good for her. She believed in most instances, love was a choice, a personal one. But this was a special case, because although Johanna never spoke directly of it, Cora believed Eric's family had helped Jenny's mother and father during the war and they were indebted to them. "It's a European story," Cora had said, leaning forward. "As an American I can't quite understand it, but I respect Johanna's experience; it must have been devastating to have been in Europe during the war." Jonas had not responded; he had let his mother talk. And now, as they walked, he refrained from mentioning either Eric or Miranda. Jenny would not have understood his relationship with Miranda; she would have expected him to have expressed more sadness, more pain—he was neither melancholy from the experience, nor had he been deeply hurt in any way. On the whole his memories of Miranda were warm and sensuous. His conflicted understanding of war, on one hand, and her poignant stridency for peace, on the other, had never interfered with their physical relationship.

He asked Jenny what her plans were for the summer, wondering if they could meet occasionally; perhaps she'd take a look at his work if she had any free time. He liked her perspective and recalled how much he had considered it while he was in San Francisco.

Jenny was reluctant to talk about her plans. All she said was that her family had decided against going to Europe this summer, but would go the next year instead. She sounded very serious, as if something else was on her mind. Then she said she'd be returning to the college soon—she attended school just outside of Philadelphia—and she would be working there for the summer; it was a clerical job, in the admissions office. He was disappointed and annoyed.

"You are sad, Jonas," she said suddenly, perceptively. He shrugged and pointed across the busy main street at the movie theater—a man in blue jeans, leaning on a ladder, was putting up letters on the marquee. A new movie would be playing that night.

They stopped walking and stared up at the marquee, cars passing before them; they watched as the man held on to the ladder with one hand and adjusted the letters with the other. "*The Day of the Jackal*," Jonas soon read. "Would you like to go?"

She turned to him and frowned, a light wind blew a loose strand of hair across her face. "Not tonight, Jonas," she said dismissively, brushing back the loosened hair.

Four

Day and Night

Ten days before, she had arrived at the station outside of Philadelphia. Early afternoon light had fallen brightly over a bouquet of daffodils left on a bench, spilling across a narrow strip of the platform and down to the tracks. The air was heavy and cool; warm sun was the only expression of spring that day. A sharp breeze pierced her cotton sweater, ruffling the collar of her blouse. Jenny shivered, turned away, and went inside the station. At the ticket counter she bowed her head and asked the woman behind the glass if the train to Boston had been delayed. "It's running thirty minutes late," she answered, her voice a monotone, her dark eyes flashing. Jenny made her way toward a chair close to the exit.

Across from her sat a couple in their early seventies, she surmised, wearing similar blue corduroy jackets. They smiled at her, their expressions mild and complacent. Jenny overheard some of their conversation and gathered they would be visiting their daughter and her family in a midsize city some miles south of Boston. Their voices calm, they apparently were not inconvenienced by the delay. But Jenny was. Impatience was something she had learned over the past year. Living away from the protection of her parents, she had come to understand it was the only way for someone like herself, an only child on her own, to hold her head above water.

In three weeks she would return to the very same train station and then would spend the summer taking classes in addition to working as a clerk in the admissions office. If she did so again the following summer, she would be able to graduate earlier than her class. It was a plan that had been in place for the last few months.

The thought of visiting her parents for even these few weeks filled her with apprehension. As she'd been preoccupied with finishing her first year of college, having just passed in her last paper the prior evening, she had not thought about the upcoming three weeks until then. She envisioned her mother bringing her morning coffee, the sun shining through the bedroom window, spotting the rattling cups and tray. Once seated on her bed, between sips of coffee, Johanna would ask in her sporadic but demanding way about her daughter's personal life. Then there was Jenny's father, his unrelenting respect for her, for her mother, for everyone he encountered, leaving for work every morning, proud yet forever humbled by the turn his life had taken.

The prior nine months had passed slowly, but there had been days when she had been jolted by the thought that midterms were a week away or the end of the semester was right around the corner. In those instances Jenny would be struck by how much she was changing, how much she already had been transformed.

As she had waved good-bye to her parents outside her dormitory the previous September, the trees still leafy and green, she had watched carefully as they climbed into their car, square-looking, a dark blue color, her father's eyes slightly misty, her mother's gaze stoic. And she had fleetingly recalled their leaving her behind the morning of her first day of kindergarten and how from the classroom window she had watched their car drive away. She had experienced a sinking within, her first sense of loss. Many Septembers later, once her father's car had vanished from sight, her heart beat fiercely, not because she had any regrets about leaving home, but because she was overcome with excitement about what was before her.

Her roommate, Arlene, salty-tongued and edgy, was petite and slim, her dark hair short-cropped, her bangs were long and full, falling past her wispy eyebrows.

Over the first few weeks they attempted to enjoy each other's company, to hopefully discover between themselves an enduring affinity. But no matter how diligently they tried, there was no connection to be found. It was not long before they mutually understood that although they would be able to tolerate living together, they would never be intimate friends. As an only child Jenny had always prided herself on her flexibility—it was the only way she'd known to get along with others. Her flexibility, she believed, benefited both of them. Arlene, the second child of five, had confided to her during those early weeks that she had learned from a young age that the more flexible she was, the more she would be taken advantage of. Whereas Jenny had learned flexibility for the purpose of acceptance, her roommate had learned to be inflexible in order to survive. Jenny believed they had understood this about each other and for that reason they had been able to last out the year together. Arlene's major was biology—she had every intention of going to medical school—and while Jenny's major was comparative literature, she had no desire like others in her field of study to eventually pursue a career in international law.

Arlene had grown up—and her family still lived—in a town only a two-hour drive from the college. She had a steady boyfriend from high school named Barry. He was attending college on a part-time basis so he could work, and he lived at home in order to save money. Whenever Arlene spoke of him, her sarcasm evaporated. As much as she could adore anyone, she adored him. Jenny soon gathered that Arlene envied what she called Barry's iconoclastic nature. One night when she was drunk, she had told Jenny that what she loved most about Barry was his fearlessness—hadn't she realized yet that most things frightened her? Jenny was studying at her desk and Arlene stood close to her; with her small hand she pushed aside her bangs and looked deeply into Jenny's eyes, unnerving her. She took quick breaths. Jenny didn't answer her directly, but told her she looked tired, that she was drunk and needed to sleep. After a few moments the tension between them dissipated; Arlene shrugged and then went to bed.

Barry would come to visit every few weekends. He was of average height but broad-shouldered, and although friendly he was not talkative. Whenever he came, Jenny would have to find another place to stay for two nights. Because the timing of Barry's visits was relatively predictable, she was able to plan in advance. But one of those weekends, a weekend when he had called Arlene in the middle of the afternoon to say he would be coming that night instead of the next Friday, Jenny did not have a place to stay. It was the second weekend in November, early evening, and Barry would be coming within the hour. Arlene anxiously paced back and forth across the room because Jenny had not yet found a place to stay. Jenny knew it was because of Barry—he was the only person she knew of who could make Arlene act in this way. She was unraveling because he was coming— any look of sarcasm or defensiveness had been wiped from her expression. Throughout the school year, it had been surprising and disconcerting to witness her change in this way.

It took Jenny a while to glean that although Arlene was an independent person intellectually and in her professional aspirations, she dreaded the thought of losing her relationship with Barry. Jenny had found this quite baffling but knew well enough not to mention it to her. Perhaps she would have if she had been a better friend, or if they had been closer.

Soon she began to pack a small overnight case with her belongings, trying to imagine who she would stay with that weekend, while Arlene stood before her in

her half-slip and bra, her arms crossed, her eyes darting, her voice tense as she made suggestions: "Caroline?
Debra? Camille?" Then there was a blunt knock and
Arlene scurried to find her skirt and sweater. Once
she had put them on Jenny carefully opened the door,
expecting to be met with Barry's impatient yet warm
gaze. But instead it was the dorm proctor, who said
that someone had come to see Jenny and was waiting
in the foyer. She thought it might be Todd, a student
from another college she had met at a mixer the previous weekend. He had said he would try and stop by on
a Friday or Saturday evening. She was pleased. She had
enjoyed talking with him. Already she was imagining
spending the evening with Todd, perhaps going out for
a pizza, then seeing a movie. Later she'd knock on the
door of a friend's room, one of the women Arlene had
suggested.

She turned away from the proctor and glanced at
Arlene, who nodded, her eyebrows knitting together
in her attempt to show concern for Jenny's situation.
Jenny put on her coat and then picked up the small case
from her bed and soon followed the proctor through the
hallway and then down the one flight of stairs to the
entrance way. As she turned the corner to walk toward
the foyer, she froze. Leaning lightly against the reception desk, his arms folded, was Eric, the worldly Eric.

He was dressed in a dark gray suit, the jacket long and fitted, a square-shaped gold clip on his moss green tie. He looked too old and foreign to be there. When he turned and caught her gaze, he lifted his eyebrows, quietly surprised. Her heart sank. How strongly she disliked him. Over the past summer she had not allowed herself to form an honest opinion of him—it had been her way of distancing herself from Eric.

He pointed to the small overnight case in her hand; she clutched it more firmly. "I have caught you at an inconvenient time—you are going home or away with a friend?" His light dismay was appealing—momentarily lessening her dislike of him.

Without flinching and with a forced confidence she explained to him about Barry's unexpected visit and told him she was planning to ask her friend in the next dorm if she could stay with her. She motioned with her free hand in the direction of the building. But when she gazed back at him he was smiling calmly, his blue-gray eyes set with an odd look of contentment. At the same time there was something about his stance, how his shoulders tensed, that made her believe he was holding himself back, that he was guarded with her. She read it as hesitation, and it relaxed her. He pressed his fingers over her hand that was pointing in the direction of her friend's dorm. Firmly lowering it, he said, "Let's have an early dinner, you can ask her later. I have a car. I've been in town on business for a week and thought I'd come by to see you before going back. I should have called to warn you . . ."

She interrupted him, asking roughly, "Did Mother ask you to check up on me, Eric?"

He looked surprised, then turned his head away and said, "I haven't spoken to your mother since I took you to dinner last August." She felt herself blush; she was not naturally caustic.

They drove into the city for dinner. It was a surprisingly warm night for mid-November. She unbuttoned her coat. From the car window she looked out at the stars. Eric was quiet and she wondered if he had something on his mind, maybe something to do with his work. She wasn't certain exactly what he did. The few times they'd been to dinner together over the summer, he'd been reluctant to talk about it. Business was what he had said, his voice sounding both determined and uneasy. She didn't know what type of business it was and he hadn't allowed her to ask about it. She was unsure if it had been out of humility on his part or embarrassment. But her mother had implied that whatever it was, it was quite a profitable business. He traveled a great deal around the country and the world. Because Jenny had been convinced ever since she met Eric that he would not be part of her future, she had not needed to know. Countless times she had told her mother that he was too old for her.

Since meeting him on the beach the previous summer, she had often wondered whether or not she had encountered him in the past. If his parents had been close friends of her parents, why had she not known of them? Or had she met his parents in their Hartford living room when she was a child? If so, had Eric been with them? She did not know. Over the summer she had attempted to bring up the subject with her mother, but Johanna dismissed her questions. "How am I to know whether or not you have seen Eric or his parents before? We know of them from Trieste. I don't speak with them often." And her mother's indifference, which Jenny believed was feigned, had made her uneasy.

Now as she studied Eric, one of his hands firmly on the steering wheel and the other relaxed on his leg, Jenny searched for any signs of familiarity. There was something recognizable about his clean-shaven face, his high cheekbones, his chin, how it subtly jutted forward, in more of an attractive than an unattractive way—as if he were graciously and perpetually trying to make one point or another. And then his crown of curly hair, incongruous with the rest of his appearance, which was cautious and neat, as were his mannerisms. "What is on your mind, Jenny? Have you had a long day?" he asked, his voice warm and cajoling, a tone he had not adopted when she had been out with him before. Over the summer he had not inferred any sort of intimacy between them and although he was not directly doing so now, in his words there was an unmistakable suggestion of it.

When he looked over, waiting for her answer, she smiled and said no more. He turned his head away and said, "You like to be mysterious, don't you, Jenny?" She heard a gentle sarcasm in his tone.

Although he'd been mostly quiet in the car, she was more surprised he was not talkative at dinner. The previous two times they had been out together as well as the day she had met him on the beach he'd been gregarious. He'd spoken mostly about how it had been for him to come to America when he was twelve years old, adjusting to the American school system, often being teased because he was European, how he believed his friends—the few that he'd made—hadn't quite trusted him, but had given him the benefit of the doubt. "You see, I was so different, Jenny," he'd said again and again. He had gone to a private high school in the city. But he had never alluded to what had happened to him after he had turned eighteen, his college and professional years. And she had not been compelled enough to ask. But this night he was different, more quiet, not asking much about her, nor speaking of himself. His eyes were steady as he perused the menu. He pointed out a certain item, pressing his finger beneath it. She noticed how well-manicured his nails were and felt both disarmed and annoyed by his obvious attention to himself. After they had placed their orders their gazes starkly met— it was as if they were at that moment exposed to each other—their hurts, their hates, their passions. But once she lowered her eyes and he, his, it was as if it had never been. He spoke first, asking if she had decided yet on a major. His English was clear, impeccable. She told him for a brief time she had considered philosophy but now was more or less settling on comparative literature. He smiled, and said, "Dante—is it because of Dante, or is it Stendhal?" his eyes glistening. She told him she had not yet read either, and that although she had read *Madame Bovary*, she had been drawn to the field not because of that novel alone but mostly because she had been compelled by the idea of comparative literature, the range of it. He smiled and said, "Ah, Flaubert—you have much to look forward to, Jenny." Briefly he closed his eyes as if trying to recall something and when he opened them, he pointedly asked, "Do you view Emma as a victim or a victimizer?"

She was surprised by his direct question, and her heart beat more quickly. "I do not think of her as one or the other—she is a romantic, but when her sense of romance takes an erotic turn, I suppose you can say she loses herself."

"Does that disturb you?" he asked, his eyes narrowing with interest.

With his wrists firmly resting on the rim of the table, his body leaning toward her, she sensed something feral about him. "Why should it disturb me?" she asked. "I am an adult."

At first he grinned, but when he answered his tone was serious. "And so you are, Jenny."

When she began to ask him where he had gone to college and what he had majored in, he diverted her attention to a woman sitting across the room who was wearing a large hat, which seemed out of place. She was facing away from them. Eric nonchalantly said he'd spent the afternoon negotiating with her and then said nothing more. Jenny did not know if he was speaking the truth, understanding it wasn't only because of his manner that she doubted what he had said, but because of her upbringing where furtiveness, secrecy, and deflection were not only taken for granted but expected. When their gazes met again, she knew they intuitively understood that about each other. She felt an inner disgust. She did not want to carry within a fear of honesty, a fear she had resented in her parents. Studying Eric, his steadfast but inscrutable eyes, the finely etched lines on his face, she wondered if he were more a citizen of Trieste. As if reading her thoughts, he asked, "You are happy to be have been born here, Jenny?"

"This is my country," she said, her voice raised. He nodded and smiled quickly. The waiter came with wine, and then food. As they began to eat, Eric asked what Trieste meant to her, if anything.

Closing her eyes, she recalled the city of her parents' births. "Gray skies, calm waters, exuberant people," she said. "That is a superficial view, but any depth I feel for Trieste has to do with my relatives there, not the city itself." He nodded, then solemnly asked if she was aware of her parents' past life in Trieste.

Hedgingly she spoke, avoiding his gaze. "I know my parents' existence in Trieste during the war is a very painful subject for them. They don't discuss it. After living with them for eighteen years, it is as if I understand their experience—it is like osmosis, I guess you could say. I know they were terrified as most were during the war. It was a traumatic experience for them. That is enough to know, I suppose. I never inquired about the day-to-day details. I never needed to. I didn't want to hurt them. If I asked too many questions, I knew I would. And there was no guarantee they would respond. Of course I've been to Trieste many times, but no one discusses the past there either. People are concerned about their current lives, the future, what is happening in their city in present time." She paused.

Eric reached across the table and grasped her hand. Their gazes locked, his pained, and for the first time she understood the depth of his sadness. He didn't say anything. Willingly she accepted his touch. He soon signaled for the waiter to bring the check. She remained silent as well.

Jenny left the restaurant, not knowing where they would be going. She understood he would not be driving her back to the college. She understood he intended to tell her about her parents' past. Deep within, she comprehended how much she needed to know.

They drove for a long while. She peered out the car window at the passing dark November night. The air was chilly now. No longer was she able to make out any stars. Eventually Eric stopped the car. She didn't know where they were; leafless trees surrounded them. She looked over at him and spoke for the first time since dinner. Despite the blackness of the night she could clearly see his blue-gray eyes. "Tell me, Eric," she said, hearing the fervency in her voice. "Tell me." Her tone frightened her; her words seemed to be coming from another person, reverberating through her, like a deep and endless echo.

It was as if she were lost in a dark forest, injured, crying out for help.

He looked away, then started the car. As he drove, she readied herself for what she was about to hear.

Within thirty minutes they were in his hotel room. After she took off her coat, he handed her a glass of brandy. Then he sat on a sofa across from her. With her free hand she gripped the arm of the chair; he explained in a dispassionate voice the details of how his parents, his family, at great risk to themselves, had protected hers during the war. And even now as she sat in the train station she could not recall his exact words. His tone was what she remembered, mostly even, descriptive, at times bitter, and between his words she had heard a begrudging acceptance. In his voice she heard truth, fear, and an unrelenting hopelessness. Though she had been in a fog as she sat there gripping the arm of the chair, she understood that Eric's father and mother, because of their standing in Trieste society, had been able to shield her parents. Her father had joined an anti-fascist group and had been active in it. He'd been interrogated twice by the authorities, Eric had said, one finger lightly stroking his chin, before his parents, close and longtime friends of her mother, had interceded to help the newly married couple.

Across from her, she now saw the elderly couple rise. She heard the train coming. When she embarked, she chose a seat near the window, leaned her head against the glass, and began to feel a sense of nostalgia about her life one year before, and about going home for the next three weeks. Although she had visited her parents twice over the school year, her time with them had been short, interrupted by visits from Eric. She had not seen them since the semester break in January. Three weeks seemed a long time now. She thought of their small home, their backyard, their busy street, Jonas's house next door. Her mother had told her he had returned that month—that he wanted to be an artist. She thought of the previous summer, his studio in the basement, his muted painting of the seagull, and the various other ones. But he seemed young now, innocent, and she had become too old. The weight of the past bore down on her, and willingly she had succumbed to its pressure. For she had learned that she could not deny what had occurred.

She and Eric did not become intimate until months later. The delay had been because his visits to the college had been sporadic. His business took up much of his time, and when they were together he spoke often and for long periods over the phone. She would go to his hotel room and fall asleep on the bed while he spoke to a colleague about one deal or another. She never paid much attention to what exactly he said, only to the relaxed insistence in his tone.

When he came to pick her up one Friday night in mid-February, she immediately realized their relationship would take another turn, would deepen. He seemed more solemn than usual. Instead of eating at a well-known and busy Philadelphia restaurant, they dined at the hotel. When they went up to his room, he did not pick up the telephone, but turned to her and said he had no calls to make that night, that unless she was opposed, they would make love completely. It had been that simple.

From that night forward, she would await his visits with a searing sense of anticipation and deep somberness. During the intervening time, she would throw herself into her schoolwork. She became more distant from Arlene, and she rarely called her mother. She wanted to hide her odd passion for Eric from them, from anyone she knew. For it was odd. She was drawn to him for reasons she did not fully comprehend—but she understood there was a darkness in her need for him, a fervency, as there was when she had begged for him to tell her about the past. A fervency she had become aware of only at that moment. And in their intimacy it was as if she was forever reliving that moment when she had pleaded with him to tell her about her parents' past. It was a feeling that stayed with her, that became more intense in her most intimate moments with Eric. He no longer seemed too old for her—they were the same. She had always been grown up in this way but had been unaware of it until then. Eric, on the other hand, had been stunted by the war. As he was a child during those years, he could only go so far. If he delved too deeply into his emotions, it would cause him too much pain; he would not be able to survive. She had come to comprehend this about him those past months, and so they had clung to each other all the more.

They had decided to marry a year from the following September. After another summer of classes, her course-work would be nearly complete. She insisted Eric go alone to see her parents, to inform them of their pending engagement. For she did not want to witness her mother's glee or her father's relief. In front of Eric they would be more subdued.

With one last thrust the train pulled into South Station. Her father would be waiting for her in the car, while her mother would be home preparing dinner. Before disembarking she took a final look out the window and was met with her own reflection. How serious she appeared, uneasy, comprehending that it was because she fully

believed Eric had not told her the complete story—
she deduced there was more. Yet in marrying him she
would be fulfilling her obligation to her parents, a real-
ization that afforded her both an added confidence and
melancholy.

Five

Sketching

When Jenny had said, "not tonight, Jonas," he had been dispirited. He had other errands to do, he had answered loosely, and said hopefully they'd run into each other again before she returned to the college. Jonas noticed a brief expression of sadness crossing her face, a warm breeze moving her fine dangling earrings. She parted her lips as if about to speak, but she didn't. He understood that she accepted his words in that disciplined way of hers and strode on.

After taking three or four steps, she turned round, as if aware he'd been watching her. When she caught his stare, he saw she had taken off her glasses. She moved closer. In the sunlight her eyes appeared more gray than brown. "Jonas," she said, her gaze penetrating his, "I knew you had left San Francisco. I am happy and pleased for you. I believe you have potential." Her voice was warm and her eyes sincere, he thought. But before he had a chance to respond she was walking at a swift pace toward her home, her form partially shaded by the passing cars.

There had been a guardedness in her voice, tempering her earnestness, a subtle warning not to pursue her. He was deflated—he found her young. Despite this, he had been hoping they would share a strong friendship. Once she disappeared from sight, he smiled ironically and thought, friendship, wasn't the joke on him?

When he got home, he went directly to the basement to work on a charcoal drawing of one of the waitresses in the coffee shop he visited every morning. From the tag on her uniform, he knew her name was Violet. He'd rise early, and would often go there with his sketch pad. One morning he had gone earlier than usual; his mother had not come home the previous night. Cora had told him, her eyes sincere and apprehensive, that she and Belinda were planning on going to a very late movie and she would be staying with her that evening. Nodding his head, his lips closed, he had understood his mother was disclosing that she'd be spending the night with Harold. When he had walked into the coffee shop that morning, no other customers were there; the coffee smelled freshly brewed, more so than usual.

He sat at the counter and soon Violet sallied over with a mug of coffee in hand. She placed it on the counter before him and began to speak as if they were old friends, revealing details about her life, her two marriages, her one child—a son, who lived mostly with his father. From time to time, her expression thoughtful, she'd twirl a strand of her hair round her forefinger. She spoke in a factual way; she wasn't inclined to feel sorry for herself. He liked that about her. In a surprisingly soft voice, pointing to the sketch pad he had placed on the counter, she asked if he was an artist. He nodded and shrugged at the same time. She seemed to accept and digest his response. Then, as if it were an afterthought, she added that she was thirty-six. He was pleased she had told him her age; he would not have guessed it— at certain moments she appeared quite young, yet she looked significantly older than her age when the light was dim.

At his desk now, his accidental meeting with Jenny no longer foremost in his mind, he switched on the lamp and began to sketch the faint lines he had noticed that morning surrounding Violet's mouth, the smallness and roundness of her eyes, the pearl-shaped irises. But he was having difficulty recalling the exact contours of her face, whether or not her cheekbones were defined or rounded, the relative distance between her lips and her chin, the width of her mouth. His desire to work that afternoon had begun to wane.

After dinner he mentioned to his mother that he had run into Jenny that afternoon. Lounging on the sofa, drinking coffee, they had been discussing the coming summer, his tentative plans—working on setting up his first exhibit by early fall—as well as her more definite ones: two weeks off in early August to visit an old friend who had moved to Texas. His mother, no longer in her work clothes, wore a pair of cotton slacks and a short-sleeved tan-colored top. In the dusky light, he studied her profile, the upward tilt of her nose, the shadows beneath her eyes.

In twenty minutes or so he would go down to his studio and work more on his sketch of Violet. Once he went downstairs Cora would either turn on the news or open the Zane Grey novel he had observed her reading the previous few days.

He had been home for two weeks and he still had not met Harold. His mother approved of his knowing about Harold, but she simply and sincerely did not want them to meet—it was his understanding that she had chosen, with a sober deliberation, to keep those two parts of her life separate. From time to time he would ponder her decision and eventually would conclude that she was preventing him from meeting Harold in order to honor the memory of his father.

When he now spoke of Jenny, Cora in her quick and exacting way placed her cup in its saucer that lay on the coffee table. Then, turning to him, her eyes startled, she said, "Jonas, I have explained to you about Jenny." His mother, appearing to have lost her natural confidence, sighed uneasily—there was a part of her that took Johanna Smila too seriously, he gleaned. He had never witnessed this uncertainty in her before, her unwavering belief in another person. She continued in a pointed and confiding voice, "There is somewhat of a mystery surrounding Johanna's family during the war and the part Eric and his family may have played in helping them. Johanna rarely speaks directly. Between the lines I have gathered there are exceptionally close and binding ties between Eric's family and Jenny's. I would not become preoccupied with Jenny. I would not be surprised if she were to marry Eric relatively soon. Johanna has not said anything conclusively, but she has alluded to the possibility." His mother looked quite serious, so much so that Jonas was filled with unease. Then she spoke again, her voice determined, though wavering some, her hands now clasped: "The past of others can hurt the innocent, the unknowing," she said. "I don't want to see you hurt, Jonas."

Annoyed with her attempt to interfere in his personal life, he firmly put his arm around her narrow shoulders, less sturdy than he expected, and said, "Don't worry, Cora, Jenny's too young for me, and Eric is too old for her." It was the first time he'd addressed his mother in this way. Initially he felt her stiffen, but soon she relaxed and met his gaze, her eyes attentive, and he felt her confidence rising. He continued, "If Eric is what Jenny wants and needs, it is a relationship I can easily accept. Friendship is all I have ever hoped for from Jenny. Today she said she would be returning to the college soon for the remainder of the summer, and so I imagine a friendship between us will not materialize." When his mother smiled warmly in response, he knew he had sounded firm and convincing. He kissed his mother on each side of her face. And with renewed energy, he hastened down the basement stairs to his studio. His memory sharper now, he worked diligently on his sketch of Violet.

He rose early as usual the next morning. When he drew apart the beige and gray curtains his mother had sewn and peered out the window, he was met with a misty day, the clouds low and heavy. The sunrise would not be visible. He quietly left the house, carefully shutting the front door. As he began his daily walk to the coffee shop, he stopped and paused in front of Jenny's home. He assumed her father would not be leaving for work for another hour and a half. All the lights were off, and there was a somberness about the Smilas' small ranch house. It was a dark brown color, and a few of the brick steps along the front path were broken, grass sprouting between the cracks. Although his home was about the same size as theirs, it seemed larger. He believed it appeared so not only because it was a pale yellow color but because of his mother. Despite Cora's small size and generally exacting nature, there was something extraordinarily large about her presence. There was a staidness about Jenny's home that saddened him. He stood there unable to move, just staring; he was overcome by an emotion he'd not experienced before—a mixed feeling of both hopelessness and hopefulness. He caught a movement in the drapes in a front window, a narrow parting. As their homes were similar in design—he had been inside Jenny's living room a few times the previous summer—he guessed it was her father checking the weather from his bedroom window. But he soon realized it was Jenny. It struck him as odd that her parents had given her the master bedroom. Only part of her face was revealed, and her long bare neck. With each hand she held on to the drapes, now bringing them closer together, shading his view of her, then suddenly she swiftly drew them farther apart. Her hair was pulled back. She was looking off into the distance as if in a trance. Her expression was both luminous and slightly degraded. Before she looked down, he began to walk quickly. He was shaken; he had been privy to another side of her, one he had not desired to know, a darker and more private side. Had the figurative mask he believed she wore, a second skin, so to speak, been at last removed and tossed aside?

He had been disoriented by Jenny's sudden appearance at her window, and so, when he stepped inside the coffee shop, he did not, as usual, seek out Violet. After a minute or two, in his search for an empty seat, he happened to glance in her direction and noticed that, despite the gray clouds, Violet appeared quite cheery, looking much younger than her age, smiling broadly. She stood behind the cash register, promptly ringing up the check of a customer.

Jonas found a vacant stool at the counter. As he rested the sketch pad on his lap, Violet approached to take his order. He made no attempt to strike up a conversation, nor did he subtly study her face in order to sketch her more accurately when he returned to his studio. Each morning he refrained from drawing her while he was at the coffee shop—he didn't want her to know he was interested in her in that way. The previous week she had noticed him sketching others who had come into the shop. She had come over and had asked to see his work, smiling slowly as she studied with a ruminative gaze what he'd been drawing.

With a few gulps he now drank his coffee, then smiled curtly at Violet, motioning to her that he was ready to pay. She appeared offended by his brusqueness; her small eyes, which he likened to two periwinkle shells half buried in a tan-colored sand, narrowed as if she were hurt. Instead of coming over to give him his check, she struck up a conversation with the customer she was serving. Eventually she came over and slapped down a check next to his empty cup. Her expression was pensive and he sensed she was deciding whether or not to converse with him.

"Where is your art pad today, Jonas?" she asked with a tinge of sarcasm, her earlier happy state having folded in his presence. She stood on her toes and peeked over the counter, pointing to it resting on his lap. "Aren't you sketching today?" she asked, her cheeks reddening. He lowered his head, ignoring her question. "You look a little pale today, Jonas," she said flatly.

As he opened the door to leave the shop, out of the corner of his eye, he saw Violet frown. He wondered if she had surmised that he had been sketching her privately. Jonas had not asked permission to do so. He'd gathered that she would not have approved—his assumption was she would have thought it a furtive activity of his.

When he returned home, his mother had already left for work. Within moments he was climbing down the basement stairs.

The studio was more untidy than usual—he did not allow his mother to clean his work area. Yet often he would become involved in sketching or painting and forget about cleaning up. Although the window was narrow, a thin layer of light wended its way into the room. The sky was no longer gray and the sun was coming from behind the clouds, the morning light picking up particles of dust.

At his desk, he switched on the lamp; the unfinished sketch of Violet lay before him. He thought it only vaguely resembled her. Instead of working more on the drawing, he put it aside. With exactitude he loosened a blank sheet from his art pad and, without a second thought, he attempted to draw Jenny. Not the Jenny he recalled from the previous summer, but the mysterious woman he discerned that morning, peering out her window, the darkness inherent in her gaze. He imagined how she would have appeared if he had been in the room with her, facing her in direct light, the drapes no longer covering the sides of her face. Pressing the piece of charcoal too firmly onto the paper, he tore into it.

Reflexively he crumpled the sheet, tossed it into the basket, and began drawing on another sheet. He sketched her eyes, the natural downward cast at the corners, then the upward tilt of her eyelids, the arch of her rounded chin, the vertical line above her lips, her high and flat cheekbones. But suddenly he stopped and stared at his work. For it wasn't remotely Jenny's likeness; instead he'd drawn a sketch of Belinda!

He held the drawing close to the light and froze. After a few minutes, his heart began to pump furiously. He could not comprehend what he'd done. What trick had his mind played on him?

Whenever he painted with a brush or worked with a piece of charcoal, he had been guided by both his hand and eye. He considered himself to be a visceral artist, one grounded in reality, more than a cerebral one. And as he knew he was not insightful in a psychological sense, he thought as he examined the sketch of Belinda he might as well have been looking at a page written in ancient script.

His mind wandered to his aunt—he had not seen her in over a year, not since she had visited him in San Francisco with his mother. At the time she'd been, and he believed still was, involved in a relationship with an ex-priest. She had seemed preoccupied during her visit, often on the phone, wrapping herself in the long springy cord. After each call, she'd tuck a five-dollar bill in Jonas's shirt pocket. He recalled her mercurial personality, how she had been the one to tell him how his parents had met, but most poignantly, the memorable conversation he had had with her in his boyhood about his father, her fine dark hair sprawled across her back, how she had tightly clutched *A Tale of Two Cities* as she spoke of David, the lone tear rolling down her cheek. Yet Jonas was aware his memories of his aunt were circumscribed; it was as if he were viewing her through a telescopic lens. He'd been a child then; he didn't know her as an adult.

With a sense of resolution, he put aside the drawing of his aunt and turned to his sketch of Violet. Although he had not paid close attention to her that morning, surprisingly, the general cast of her features was now fresh in his mind. Thoughts of the change in Jenny and his inadvertent sketch of Belinda slipped from his consciousness; he became absorbed in the drawing. For he was envisioning the contours of Violet's face more and more clearly. Soon he was immersed in his work.

He did not speak to Jenny again during her three-week visit that May. And other than that early morning at the window, he'd noticed her only one other time. It was at the movie theater, about a week after he had seen her at the drugstore. It took him a while to realize it was Jenny. It was a cool night, and she wore a dark green sweater. She sat five rows in front of him, next to Eric, Jonas assumed. He had not seen Eric before, but because of Jenny's detailed description of him the previous summer, he was easily recognizable.

Jonas was alone. He had considered asking Violet that morning—she had become friendlier over the last few days—but he was skittish about becoming involved in a serious relationship with anyone. On some mornings Violet would ask to see his sketches and then comment on them and make suggestions after she guessed which customer he was drawing. She once asked if he needed to ask permission to draw a person. He told her he didn't know what the ethics of an artist was, but it was only a sketch, his impression of the person, so it didn't really matter. She seemed to ruminate over what he had said but had not responded.

He studied Eric, who wore a jacket with a collared shirt and no tie. He recalled Jenny's haunting expression as she had stood peering out the window that morning a week before. Her body leaned in Eric's direction while he sat straight, looking up at the screen. From time to time she'd raise her hand to the back of his neck and stroke it, but Eric did not take her hand nor did he put his arm around her.

After a while Eric rose from his seat and walked up the aisle. Jonas saw Jenny turn to watch, her eyes solely on Eric. Because of the dim lighting, Jonas could not decipher the expression in her eyes. It was more of her posture, her doting on Eric, that disturbed him. For she had always come across to him as quite independent. His past interactions with her briefly crossed his mind. He thought of how she'd examine his paintings, not really caring if she was overly critical. Or how she stayed away from him whenever she was with her friends and he had been invited to come along. It had taken him a while to realize she had invited him out of politeness, that she really did not want him around when she was with her friends. She had preferred to be alone with him. Jonas thought that with him she invariably had the upper hand. But that night she was not the Jenny he had known the previous summer. He wondered if there was more to their relationship, a pending marriage, as his mother had implied. Although Jenny appeared cool and contained, she was quite caring and he believed she would be protective toward anyone she considered to be a friend or a lover. Because of this it was difficult to determine what she desired, which direction in life she would choose. Then, uneasily, he thought of her at the window that morning, her haunting presence.

When Eric returned to his seat, Jonas noticed a stealthy yet upbeat agility in his walk that was so inharmonious he found it jarring. Jenny didn't look in Eric's direction; she now seemed to be completely absorbed by the movie. But once Eric sat next to her she turned to him. There was something about the movement of her head, her profile in silhouette, that caused Jonas to sense a pleading in it. He was disquieted, and he diverted himself by focusing on the movie, a movie whose title he would never recall.

What he would remember was that it was a movie about an older woman in her late forties and a younger man who was approximately thirty years old. It might have been a French movie, which from time to time would come to their small city. But he was not certain whether or not he had to read subtitles that night. The couple meet at a party and she at first speaks to him in a somewhat maternalistic way, chides him for spilling his coffee as she watches over him at the dessert table. Then she shows him how to pour it properly, holding the pot higher, not close to the cup. Neither of them speak; it is all explained through movement and shaking of the head or nods. The younger man shrugs it off; he isn't chagrined by her instruction—he is a poet. With filled coffee cup in hand, he leaves her and walks confidently across the room to speak with a young woman who obviously admires him. Jonas would not remember more about the plot, but he'd recall that a short time later the late-forties woman and the thirty-year-old poet were in bed together.

From his point of view, the movie paralleled his perception of the relationship between Eric and Jenny. During the film, his eyes would often stray from the screen to the two of them. But the more the movie progressed, the more Jenny and Eric seemed immersed in it.

When the film was over, Jonas lowered his head as Jenny and Eric made their way up the aisle toward the exit. When he thought they had passed his row, he cautiously raised his eyes. They had come to a standstill; the couple in front of them was immersed in conversation with another couple and they were blocking Jenny and Eric from moving forward. Jonas lowered his head again, yet his gaze drifted left and he was met with the sight of their hands, how urgently Jenny pressed Eric's, which were behind his back, both of hers clutching his. He had no need to worry that she might notice him; she was fixated on Eric. Her eyelids were lowered, heavy— as if she were drugged.

Eric, Jonas thought, appeared indifferent to Jenny's adoration of him. He accepted it, Jonas concluded, as he would have expected a delicious dinner at a well-known restaurant or a nearly flawless gem at a prestigious jewelry store.

By the time Jonas left the movie theater and was walking toward home, the two of them were no longer in his thoughts. As a couple, they were not an uplifting sight. They were a heavy sort, he decided—he did not perceive the seesawing from banality to excitement he noticed in the relationships and marriages of his friends.

Despite how uneasy he had felt observing Jenny and Eric, when Jonas returned home that evening he felt a strong sense of renewal. He knew that all he wanted now was to paint, to draw. Painting and drawing soothed him, distracted him from the dissonance in humanity. His natural irony and tendency to be skeptical could no longer shade him from darker realities; he was turning more and more to art.

He found his mother sitting quietly, staring at the blank screen of the television set. In her lap was a book. Jonas went to her and put his arm around her, wondering if she and Harold had had an argument. He fleetingly recalled how as a young boy he'd touch her hair whenever he had come upon her sleeping. He had an urge to do so now, out of habit, nostalgia. But she seemed solemn. "Jonas," she said softly, smiling warmly. He knew at that moment she was not sad and that things were probably fine with Harold, that maybe she had been savoring her general sense of contentment. Jonas told her he was hoping not to be living with her too much longer, maybe a year at the most. He needed to be independent. He was twenty-eight.

She looked steadily at him, pursed her lips, and then said, "I understand, Jonas."

That night he dreamed of Jenny; the man she was with was not Eric, but the man he had seen in the coffee shop, who he'd thought might be Harold.

About a year later, during one of his trips to New York, Jonas thought he spotted Jenny and Eric. Jenny had not planned to come home that summer, his mother had told him, as she would be getting married in early September. Eric and Jenny, he believed, were in front of a clothing store on Madison Avenue, but he wasn't certain it was them. He was coming up the street—he had just been at the Metropolitan nearby. The woman who he thought might be Jenny was pointing to something in the window and the man she was with was looking in the opposite direction. Then they disappeared inside the store. By the time Jonas got there and went inside, they were nowhere to be found. He rushed out and looked up the street, but they were not in sight. He could not fathom how they could have gone in and then come out without his seeing Jenny and Eric, as his eyes had been glued on the store ever since he had first noticed them. Then he wondered if it had been his imagination, after all.

His mother received an invitation to Jenny's wedding. It would take place in Milan so that both Jenny's relatives and Eric's family could come from Trieste. Eric had wanted a honeymoon on the Riviera, according to what Johanna had told his mother, a sort of an apologetic explanation for having it so far away.

Jonas had gathered that the Smilas no longer had many friends in the United States and that most, like Eric's parents, had returned to Trieste. They had come to America to escape memories of the war and, to an extent, to be reborn—but it had been difficult to achieve a sense of renewal, and so they had returned. Because of Jenny, he knew, the Smilas had stayed.

His mother was indecisive. Harold—whom Jonas still had not met—was, according to his mother, not interested in attending. Cora, who had not been to Italy before, was becoming more and more intrigued about the possibility of seeing the country of her ancestors. She looked at Jonas as if considering whether or not to ask him. That is when he suggested Belinda. "Belinda no longer likes to travel," she said, surprised that he had mentioned her as a possibility. He recalled his sketch of his aunt the previous year, and felt discomforted.

Eventually his mother convinced Harold to attend. Following the wedding they would spend a few weeks traveling around the country. Harold had agreed to go as long as they made a side trip to Liverpool, where his grandparents had been born. Jonas was occupied with an upcoming exhibit of his work at the gallery he had worked in two summers before.

When his mother returned from the trip she spoke about their travels, but not of the wedding. A few months later she introduced Jonas to Harold; she left them alone while she went out Christmas shopping. Harold and he had a superficial chat, but after shaking hands before they parted, they both knew they had no interest in knowing more of each other. Harold left before Cora had returned from her shopping excursion.

During the time Jonas lived with his mother, she never brought Harold to their home to spend the night. He didn't at all resemble the man Jonas had seen in the coffee shop. And after meeting Harold, he rarely saw him—only if he was coming to pick up his mother or driving her home—yet whenever his name was mentioned Jonas would envision not the actual Harold, but the man in the coffee shop he had imagined to be him.

Jonas lived in his mother's home for a few months short of two years, and left in early 1975. He had just turned thirty years old. He'd had a few exhibitions of his paintings at galleries downtown, but his art was not supporting him. Through the contacts he had made during what had become his monthly trips to New York, he had been offered a job as a portrait artist at an upscale art gallery.

Although he would be painting people of means, at least he would be painting, not selling, and he'd continue his own independent work as well.

He regretted that he had not had a chance to see Harold and his mother interact. All he knew of them as a couple was that vague conversation he had overheard the night he had spent in the basement three years before. He had often thought that if he had observed his mother and Harold together for a certain amount of time, he would have understood something about his parents' marriage or how she might have appeared with his father. His mother could not have possibly known how much he had wanted her to marry Harold or at least live with him. And in terms of Jenny's marriage to Eric—Jonas was bewildered. When he left for New

York, he had no sense of what the true meaning or purpose of marriage was. No longer retaining the idealized
vision of his parents' relationship he had as a boy, he
instead carried with him the dry and stilted definition of
marriage he'd read again and again, as a young adolescent, late at night, in his mother's old Webster.

Six

Summer and Fall

Summer heat, intense and persistent, filled her with a
sense of longing. In her dormitory room, at her desk,
book in hand, she peered closely at the text, the whir-
ring fan close to her emitting soft, warm air. The words
on the page did not appear clear and crisp, nor did the
characters seem as strong and vibrant as the subjects she
had analyzed and written about during the school year;
instead they were hazy, as if she were viewing them from
a distance, across a murky pond, the sun in her eyes. They
were blurred and undefinable. It was becoming more and
more challenging to keep her coursework foremost in her
mind. The papers she wrote were rambling and unfocused. Her emotions superseded her intellect.

The summer of 1973, she took four courses—two in the first summer session, occurring mostly during the month of June, and two in the second, which began after the fourth of July and ran through the second of August. She would study late at night when at times it was cooler—though many evenings the heat was unbearable. Then she would get up from her desk, go to the open window, and stare out at the still grounds of the campus. Usually no one was in sight. One night Jenny spotted a woman who worked with her in the office, her supervisor. She was strolling across the campus, holding hands with a man Jenny recognized as a security guard in the main building. He was much younger than she was. Jenny could not clearly see their faces until they walked beneath the lights of her dormitory—how loosely they moved, how ecstatic their expressions.

There were moments when she'd ask herself why she had bothered to take classes over the summer. What was the rush? She'd be married in September of the following year; she planned to take that semester off, then return in the spring to complete her coursework. Yes, what was the rush? Others had questioned her plans; those who worked with her in the admissions office were surprised she had set up such a rigorous schedule. What was the purpose?

~

A few weeks later, Eric surprised her, showing up unexpectedly in her office to take her to lunch. She had not seen him in nearly a month. Over the summer she had arranged her work schedule around her classes. Now that her summer studies were complete, she worked in the office full time.

It was an early August day, and although the temperature was over ninety degrees, Eric wore a gray linen suit that accentuated his blue-gray eyes. When he stepped into the office their gazes met and she said, "I missed you." The words escaped her lips like a soft sigh. No one else was working at the noon hour, but she knew she would have said it regardless. He had wanted her to finish her coursework—he had no intention of distracting her, he'd said the last time she saw him. Then he had disappeared until that day. His expression was impassive as she spoke, but that was his way and she was never quite certain what he was feeling beneath the surface—only when they were in bed together. It was the only time his feelings would be aroused, when she experienced his anguish. It was as if she held power over him when he cried. And she would hold him close, ask what was causing him such pain; she would run her finger across his forehead then down his nose to his mildly pointy chin until his eyes were dry.

Over lunch he told her about his travel plans for the next year, where he would be going until their wedding in early September. It was only thirteen months away, he said, matter-of-factly; he was never one to be emphatic.

"Are you happy, Jenny?" he asked suddenly, his gaze both hopeful and distant. She heard a touch of irony in his tone. They sat outdoors, and the sunlight caught the gold of his cuff links and she again noted his manicured nails. She looked at him steadily, thinking how she had not considered happiness, but obligation, since meeting him. She felt agitated. The waiter came to pour more water into their glasses and Eric was diverted. When they were alone again, she turned the question to him. "How could I not be happy, Jenny?" he responded so simply that, raising the water glass to her lips, she felt her pulse quickening.

Although he had told her where he would be traveling over the next eleven months, he had not told her why he would be going to Madrid or Tel Aviv or London. He did not tell her about his business, and it did not occur to her to ask. She was certain her mother and father knew. If it was something untoward, they would not have encouraged her to be with him, they would not be so overjoyed by their engagement. She trusted him, she trusted them. There was no point in not doing so. During the school year, she relished her coursework, her plans for a career—outside her passion for Eric, it was her sole interest.

Eric was more intrigued by her classes than she was his business. She now told him about the two courses that ended the previous day. One was a comparison of Svevo's *Zeno's Conscience* and Joyce's *Ulysses*. He smiled. It pleased him whenever she spoke of literature, especially European. He asked her what she would like do after she graduated. They had agreed not to have children for ten years. He was not ready and neither was she. She told him she might teach. What else was there to do with a degree in comparative literature? "Compare, I suppose," he said, jokingly.

"Compare what?" she asked, smiling. He leaned across the table and whispered a sexual comment, which she shrugged off; it had dampened the carefree mood between them, she thought.

Eric would be in town for the next ten days. He would be meeting with clients in Philadelphia, and then a week holiday on Maui together would follow. He wanted her to be refreshed before she began her second year of college. She was apprehensive; they had not spent this much time together before. While he was in town, she would go to his hotel every night and he would drive her to work the next morning.

She preferred Eric's luxurious hotel to her dormitory room; in the lobby there were huge sparkling chandeliers and thick handmade rugs, mostly a deep red color. When Eric wasn't looking, she'd slip off her sandal and touch the carpet with her bare foot; she'd experience a thrill within, the arch of her foot pressing into the sensual texture of the carpeting, and she'd reflect on where she had come from, how young she was, how much of life there was before her.

She sensed it would be different with Eric now. Not having been in his company for a month, she noticed a certain edginess in him that hadn't been apparent to her before. And over lunch when he had made the sexual comment, she had been surprised; she hadn't believed he was inclined to such talk in her presence. But now as they rode the elevator to the room she chalked it up to her own lack of experience, her naïveté. She did not love him less, but only more—she appreciated the many sides to him. Whereas at first she thought his remark had dampened the communication between them, by the time they were walking down the hallway toward his room, she believed it would make their intimate moments more complex. She was both somber and elated.

Once inside the room, he locked the door, then turned to her and beckoned her to come to him. Their gazes met; gingerly she approached. He pressed her close, so close she could barely catch her breath. Suddenly he released her. When she looked up at him, there was an expression crossing his face she had not been aware of before. She was accustomed to his sadness, his mournfulness when they had made love in the past. Now she witnessed a strictness, how he lifted his chin. Yet she trusted him.

"What is it, Eric?" she asked, meeting his gaze, noticing strands of brown in his irises. She was not able to read or interpret his intention. Her eyes rested on the shadows beneath his eyes. She knew he had been working late and was under much pressure, as businessmen are during certain months. He had mentioned to her before that late summer was a stressful time for him. She had been surprised that he had arranged the trip to Maui, but then had assumed it was because of his work.

"Nothing in particular, Jenny. I know you are quite independent and would not have any qualms about walking away from me, breaking our engagement."

Her heart pounded; she again met his gaze. "Do you want to break our engagement, Eric? I am confused. Do you not love me, do you want us not to be together?" Her imaginings of their future life together began to scatter in her mind like autumn leaves falling prematurely from a tree.

He embraced her again, with more caution now; her face rested against his chest. She was not able to see his expression. "Let's take a walk," she heard him say. His voice sounded somewhat distant, as if coming from a television or radio in the next room.

She stepped away from him, her hands still on his arms. "If you need to speak, Eric, I'd prefer you do so in this room." She was forcing herself to say those words; within she was uncertain. It was a new experience for her.

He smiled and said, "Jenny, you always surprise me. Sometimes you appear confident and composed and at other times young and naïve."

Shaken, she went and sat on the edge of the bed and tightly closed her eyes, not from sadness but as a way of gathering herself, readying herself for a deeper strength she knew she would need to reveal. She was keenly aware of the difference in their ages and how because of it he held much knowledge and experience of the world over her. Worldly Eric, she thought with deep irony. It struck her that honesty, her newly developed frankness, was what she possessed, was what would help her counter his experience.

When she looked up, his back was to her. He stood near the window; he had pushed aside the drapes and was looking out. She wondered how much she would be able to comprehend what he had experienced during the war.

He turned to her and said, "We are different, Jenny, maybe too different." Their gazes met; his was determined. She forced herself to speak.

"What is wrong, Eric? What has happened since we were last together? I will not stay with you if you believe we are so different." She pulled off her engagement ring and placed it on the table next to the bed. "I will go, Eric. You are free now. We are no longer engaged." She read amazement in his eyes. This was not what he had expected from her. Or was his expression of amazement his way of hiding how startled he felt? Startled by his own words? Did he think he had so much control over her? Tears began to gather in his eyes.

"Don't leave, Jenny."

"What happened this past month, Eric, that makes you this way—so committed at one moment, so distant at the next?"

No longer melancholic, he appeared strained, unsure. She continued, "Or was it much before that? What are you not telling me, Eric?" His name coming from her lips sounded sharp and constricted.

120

He went to the door and she believed he would leave her now. She was getting too close. He stood at the door. She knew he was not certain. She understood him only through her parents, their life—that was the root of her comprehension. Closing her eyes, she took a deep breath—it was one of indecision. She was not sure whether or not their engagement should continue. It was a moment of uncertainty for both of them. Who was more unsure? Who was more reliable? Which one of them was less destructive? Directness had been a struggle for her most of her life. She had been taught to be evasive.

His hand gripped the doorknob. Her heart pounded. Fleetingly, she imagined her life with him and then without his presence. Which was more promising? The many trips to Europe, his love, having his children? Or her complete independence, her freedom? Then she thought of her parents and was convinced she would never be free—for her, freedom was an illusion. She honored their experience during the war. Would she ever be able to shake herself from its bonds?

Eric turned to her. He had taken his hand off the doorknob. She could not read the expression in his eyes that were now clear, not one trace of unshed tears. "Take the ring," she said, pointing to the table next to the bed. He came to her and lowered her hand.

"I want us to be married."

"No doubts?" she asked.

"None whatsoever," he said. But though his voice was firm and assured, his eyes were distant. Yet it was his low and confident voice that reached her. Its sound caressed her like a warm high wave engulfing her. She threw her arms around his waist and he kissed her with a disquieting fortitude.

"A lovers' argument," she said, gazing up at him, hearing how hollow her voice sounded. He ran his hands down her back; there was an impatience in his touch.

He nodded, his eyes slightly less distant. In this moment he was with her, she believed.

It was a little after midnight. Rustling sounds filled the room; in the darkness they made their way to the bed. They had just come in from a very late dinner, five courses, much wine. Eric's intention had been to celebrate their being together again after a month separation. He had not anticipated their argument, their near breakup. Since they'd been together they had not argued, until that day. Eric had not had as much wine as Jenny had. He was careful never to drink too much; he was always on alert, it seemed. He was always in control, and she understood this about him, as she was not so dissimilar. Tonight though, from the tension of the near breakup of their engagement, from her uncertainty, she had allowed herself to open up more, to not be aware of how many glasses of wine she'd drunk.

On the drive back to the hotel, her words slightly slurred, she had teased him, chided him about his pointy chin, like an orchestra conductor's. He was smiling in the dark, a relaxed smile, highlighted as they passed beneath a street light and then lights from an oncoming car. "Jenny, Jenny," was all he had said. Despite his mostly impassive expression, she had heard unbounded relief in his voice. It had been wonderful to tease him. She believed they were closer now. Their disagreement, their near separation had been worth it, she thought.

In the dark she slipped out of her clothes and tumbled into bed. Silence. Soon she realized Eric was no longer with her; he was not in the room. She lay in bed waiting. Forty minutes later the door cracked open. He did not switch on the light. She could see him in silhouette, undressing. Then she felt his weight next to her in the bed. Within moments he had turned his back to her. She stared up at the ceiling, a blank white sheet, as the night passed into morning.

∼

It was early September, the first week of her sophomore year of college. Her life at school was different than it had been the previous year, mostly because she did not have a roommate. Arlene had transferred to a state school closer to her home, and Jenny had not found out until the week before. She had been disappointed Arlene was no longer at the college. She would miss their eclectic conversations. Arlene had enhanced her life in that she had been her only experience with a sibling of sorts. Jenny had called her a few times, but after exchanging initial pleasantries Arlene was always in a rush. She did not want to talk more. Jenny assumed this was her way of coping with their separation, and she understood there would be a day when they would no longer communicate.

Others did not approach her as much as they had the previous year. A classmate might ask her what the homework assignment was for the next day, or when the next paper would be due. Women suspiciously eyed the engagement ring on her finger and it was noted that she had her own dorm room. She was considered mature. She was no longer truly part of the college environment. She was like a shadow of a student whose essence was elsewhere.

Her thoughts were mixed about her new status. At times she felt more sophisticated and knowledgeable than other students. In class, she spoke out, neither too much nor too little, but with confidence, and only to make a particular point. She was now an experienced woman who had known love and passion, who had her career before her with a successful fiancé at her side. She was no longer thought of as naïve Jenny.

She often asked herself if she missed those early months the previous year when school was first beginning, before Eric had walked into her life. Yet as much as she tried, she could not bring those days to mind, or recall the early excitement. Perhaps she had locked away the experience because it simply was not relevant to her life any longer. She was not dismayed or even reminiscent. She thought first of her present reality, and then she'd remind herself that her parents would no longer exist if Eric's family had not intervened, and how in their doing so, they had allowed her to be.

Her path in life was very clear. Did she love Eric out of a sense of filial duty? Whenever she asked herself this question, she understood it was unknowable. Her situation was complex and involved—any attempt to answer such a question would sound insincere and perhaps even false. Someday she hoped she would have the maturity to comprehend why she loved Eric, why she was committing herself to him. Although he was older, she believed she was the more grounded one. She hesitated to ask him about his days as a child in Trieste during the war. She did not know how much he remembered. He had dreams of horror. She'd hear him call out in his sleep. His cries would awaken her and she'd sit up in bed and watch over him; she'd wait until his sleep was again sound. In his conscious life, his life unburdened from his dreams, she believed he had no awareness of his childhood. He had shut those days out of his life as she had drawn a shade over her carefree days when she had believed so profoundly in her independence. His method of shutting down the past was unconscious, while hers was accomplished in full awareness.

She had attempted to research Trieste, what had happened during the war, the anti-fascist group her father had been part of, but she had not been able to unearth much; it still was an enigma to her, and so not quite real. All she knew was that Italy had declared war on Nazi Germany, October 1943. Her imagination roughly filled in the rest. She had come to understand that Eric, other than that night he had first spoken of it, mirrored her parents in that it was a subject he did not want to approach, let alone discuss. She understood why he had been compelled to reveal the truth; he had needed her to be cognizant of her parents' past and their connection with Eric and his family. Yet he had not said more. Their linkage had become nonverbal—it had been evident in his lovemaking, which ran the gamut from high emotion to detachment and distance. On her part it was evidenced in her devotion to Eric, or at times her dispassionate objectification of him. There were days when she would wonder if it was possible that she hated him. But she would remind herself she had never hated anyone.

It was the end of the first week of September, 1974, and they had been married for seven days. They would spend another week on the French Riviera, heading to the Italian side the following Saturday. It was wonderful to lie on the beach. Although the air was only slightly cooler at this time of year, the sun was strong, beating down relentlessly over their half-naked bodies. She had never before felt such a surge of physical strength and well-being as in those days by the sea.

Two nights before, Eric had disappeared for a few hours, but was back in their room by eleven. That night his lovemaking had been hasty, less inclusive, and she had felt like a bystander. The next morning she was uneasy and doubts started to creep into her mind about their marriage. But the previous night after they had spent the entire day together, he had been as caring and as romantic as his nature would allow, fully revealing his melancholy when they made love. It was at these times when she most understood Eric. When he disappeared for a few hours, which he had for two nights of their week-old marriage, she had been uneasy. She had no idea where he was. When he returned, she'd ask him where he'd been. He'd avoid answering her directly. He had his contacts in Europe, he'd say. And she would tell herself he was seeing his business associates, as he had indicated he might before their wedding. But she never fully believed him. She was beginning to understand there was a part of Eric she would never know. That was where their age difference asserted itself. While she was a young child, he had begun to establish these contacts. It was his world without her. Although she knew she must allow him to live it, given who she was she did not believe it would be possible for her to easily do so. Was that the sacrifice expected when there was an age difference such as theirs? Was it a sacrifice she would not be able to make? For when she had asked him where he was, his response had always been the same: "Business—I can't stop working because we are enjoying a very long honeymoon. I am not that wealthy, Jenny." There had been neither scorn nor pleading in his voice; his tone had been low and factual.

That night she lay alone in bed. Her back was badly sunburned. It was difficult to fall asleep. The windows were open and there was a caressing breeze. When Eric was not with her, she liked to listen to the rush of the waves.

Above the sound of the ocean, she now heard people talking on the terrace, the clattering sound of waiters clearing dishes and silverware from the tables on the patio just below. It was a small, intimate restaurant— the ocean a stone's throw away—with round tables and white linen tablecloths, a candle and a vase with one flower adorning the center of each one, waiters in white jackets scurrying about.

It was one o'clock in the morning. She experienced a sense of contentment, the scenery, the night, the light conversations below. It was idyllic. Then she thought of her marriage and her feeling of wholeness dissipated. For a moment she wished Eric would only be the Eric she preferred and that they would live this life forever, that they would not go home. She closed her eyes wishing. But then she thought of home, of school, which she would again attend in January, and she knew they must return. They would be living in Philadelphia then. That was what belonged to her, her schoolwork; it represented her life, her future as an independent person, as independent as she could possibly be.

She heard voices from below again, louder now, a conversation. There were many people talking. Three or four men, two or more women, she thought. They were from various places, she gathered, as they had different accents, though they were all speaking English. From time to time one lapsed into French, and then another person would respond in French but soon they were all speaking English again. They were too far away—she could not determine their exact words or what they were speaking of.

Slowly it dawned on her that one of the voices was Eric's. His tone was different. He was laughing and he sounded as young as the others. She was accustomed to his subdued and at times stern voice, ever confident. She had always thought this was because of his age. Yet now she heard how young he was. She imagined him sitting out on the patio, wearing blue linen pants and a white cotton shirt with the sleeves rolled up—how he was dressed when she had parted from him in the early evening, just before he had slid into the car he was renting, telling her he had to meet with an old client and wasn't certain when he'd be back.

Now she heard his laughter, his light tone, and for a fleeting moment she was hopeful. Then she heard chairs scraping against concrete.

Ten minutes later Eric walked into the room. She heard him place the key on the table next to the bed. She pretended she was sleeping, though her heart beat wildly. He sat next to her. "Wake up, Jenny," he said, urgently. She smelled alcohol on his breath. Her eyes opened. He leaned over and switched on the light. As he got up, she felt his weight leave the bed. Standing now, he slowly undressed, his leg grazing her bare arm.

In Lucerne the dark mystique of Halloween hissed throughout the city. The weather was quite cool. During the day, the sky was mostly gray. Their hotel room looked out over the turbulent river that snaked through the city; its covered bridges appeared more white against the dusky sky.

The next day they would begin their trip back to the United States. Those few days in this old city marked the end of their two-month honeymoon. It had been one of highs and lows, and she was not certain if their marriage would be a successful one. She had learned that Eric was erratic, to say the least: kind and emotional at one moment, stern and demanding at the next. Fortunately she had been able to ignore his spurious wants, diverting him whenever possible, never succumbing to him when he was so inclined. At such times their relationship devolved into a seemingly endless game of dodgeball.

It was now close to five o'clock. They walked through the streets, not holding hands as they would have during the early days of their trip. Each of them gazed off in another direction—she was searching for she knew not what; Eric's stare was with purpose. He stopped in front of a department store and, without turning toward her, said he needed to go inside. They would be attending a Halloween party at their hotel that night, and she knew he was looking for a hat that would go with his costume. She sat outside on a bench across from the entrance; she preferred the cool evening air more than the hassle of shopping in a large store. Her mind drifted to the uncertainties of the past two months and again she wondered if their marriage would last. She rationalized that it was too early to know; they had many years before them to discover more about each other. On the other hand, their marriage was fraught with complications—in particular, Eric's inability to talk in any depth about his work. Although she had not insisted on knowing much—she had put her trust in her parents' judgement—she had lately begun to ask direct questions about what he did, especially since he'd been disappearing for hours. When he'd return, he'd expect her to react as if he'd been away for only twenty minutes or so.

He would appear surprised by her questions; he felt he didn't need to answer in any depth, because he would provide for her. He told her she only needed to know specifics if his business for some unknown reason took a turn for the worse. She was relieved they would not have children for a while. Given the difference in their ages, having a child now would be difficult; they had much ground to catch up on before they would be ready for that step.

They were an hour late to the Halloween party. She was dressed as a shepherdess and Eric was a pirate—not a very compatible pair. She was wrapped in a white sheet, one shoulder exposed, her hair in a loose ponytail that reached down to the center of her back. She held a staff in one hand. Eric had a black patch over his eye and he wore a short red jacket and black pants. He had not been able to find an appropriate hat at the department store.

When she glanced across the room, her pulse quickened; she had spotted a familiar form, a woman, standing next to the buffet table. Without thinking she began to approach her, her heart pounding. The woman wore a black mask and was dressed like a feline. Pausing for a moment, Jenny turned back to look for Eric. She did not see him. She was not certain where he had gone.

Her curiosity was boundless. She felt slightly dizzy as she walked toward this familiar form; the lights in the large room seemed to blend together and shimmer. Now she was next to her. The woman turned to her; she was holding a glass of wine in one hand, a canapé in the other. Jenny did not say anything, only peering into the familiar eyes. The woman put down her glass, and with one swift motion, she removed her mask. "Arlene! Why are you here?" Jenny cried out, her heart in her throat. Before Arlene answered, Jenny looked quickly about the room, but she did not see Eric. It was as if he had been consumed by the crowd. Her hand on her forehead, she felt how moist it was. She looked again at Arlene. She was smiling now. She had always liked the element of surprise, Jenny thought, recalling how Arlene would disappear on certain nights and would not tell her the next day where she'd been. She'd leave unexpectedly and return in the same mysterious way. Jenny had never known whether or not to report to the dormitory proctor that Arlene was missing.

"Semester abroad," she said now, her lips moving in an exaggerated way, perhaps because there was a density about the room; although no one was talking loudly, there was a sense that if you spoke, you would not be heard.

"In Lucerne?" she asked skeptically.

"Zurich," Arlene answered again with her lips.

Jenny's eyes filled with tears. She turned away to search again for Eric. All she saw were the tops of heads, some with odd-shaped hats that she imagined suited their costumes, and then cigarette smoke trailing just below the ceiling. It seemed she had lost Eric. When she looked back at Arlene, she noticed that her face was flushed. Arlene picked up her wine glass and as she sipped from it, she looked askance at Jenny. She noticed an engagement ring on Arlene's finger. "So you are engaged," Jenny said, nervously. "Barry?"

She shook her head. "I met someone in Zurich, a banker."

"That was fast," Jenny said in a noncommittal way, her heart thumping.

"I suppose you could say we fell in love." As Arlene spoke, her eyes were nearly vacant. It was as if she was a different person with a different spirit in the form of Arlene.

"Is he here?"

"Yes, he is a friend of Eric's. I think they have gone off somewhere."

"A friend of Eric's? How did you meet him?" Jenny felt herself shaking within, thinking how odd it was for Arlene to be in Lucerne, to be engaged to a friend of Eric's—more strange than anything she had witnessed or experienced with Eric.

Arlene looked at her in that old way of hers. And for a moment Jenny felt a sense of familiarity—it was as if they were back in their college dorm room. "Life is full of coincidences," Arlene said, gulping down the remainder of her drink.

Jenny looked away and spotted Eric across the room, deep in conversation with a man she assumed was Arlene's fiancé. He was evidently older than Eric. And Jenny thought of the young and vibrant Barry and how heartbroken he must have been when Arlene had announced she was engaged to someone else. Those early days with Eric during her first year of college flashed across her mind, and then she looked again at Arlene. Arlene had always seemed a backdrop to their relationship. She had only seen Eric briefly that first year of college, on three or four occasions, and had not appeared to be impressed in the least with him. Jenny had thought she was always comparing him in her mind to Barry, and she had assumed Eric was the one who had come up short. Arlene had let Jenny know in subtle ways that she believed Eric was too old for her—especially when she emphasized how wonderful it was to be involved with someone her own age. And here Arlene was now with a much older man, older than Eric.

A sudden surge of strength bolstered Jenny; she was not as naïve as she had been when she had lived with Arlene. No longer did she hazily, dreamily think there was more to Eric's story; she knew there was, in a way she had not fathomed.

Seven

Winter

On a bitterly cold Saturday morning, late December, 1980, Jonas learned of Eric Stram's death. For an hour he had been sitting near the door in a coffee shop on Seventh Avenue, assailed by a draft of cold air each time someone came in or left. His table faced an ice-framed window; he peered out at the bleak scene, the malaise of winter encroaching upon the city. The sky was colorless, and pale, vacant expressions clouded the faces of the pedestrians.

He forced himself to consider his future. The new year was a few days away, and in a month, he'd turn thirty-six. There was something of significance about that age; it was a marker of where one was, what one had achieved. Should he continue on as he had for the last while or should he turn his career and life in another direction?

More than five years earlier, he had come to New York and he still was uneasy there, though he grudgingly acknowledged he'd never felt attuned to any setting—not in the small college environment in western Massachusetts where he had spent the first four years of adulthood, nor in the years he had lived in San Francisco as a middling art salesman. And in terms of his home close to Boston, even as a young boy he'd viewed it as a place-in-waiting.

The man at the next table who had not removed his knit cap the entire time he'd been there suddenly got up and left; the newspaper he'd been reading was sprawled across the Formica-topped table. Reflexively Jonas's gaze wandered over and he noted at the top of a page Eric Stram's name in bold dark letters. As it was early he was still sleepy and so at first the name didn't register. He looked away and then spotted a woman crossing the street who he thought seemed familiar, perhaps someone he had painted, but realized within seconds that he'd not seen her before. And then his gaze wandered

back to the newspaper and up to the name of Eric
Stram, and at that moment it dawned on him that Eric
Stram was Jenny's Eric. Jonas got up and snatched up
the newspaper; clutching it with both hands, he stood
and read the article with a mingling of intensity and
dispassion.

What he determined from his first read through
was that Eric's death had been an accident, but there
was no description nor any details about the accident.
"Successful businessman," Jonas read; but there was no
clarification of what business he was in. Jenny was mentioned only at the very end along with his parents, who
were living in Trieste, Italy, as his survivors. No other
siblings were mentioned but Jonas vaguely recalled having heard from either his mother or Jenny that Eric had
had an older brother who had died during the Second
World War. He also noted that Eric had passed away
six weeks before. He wondered why his mother had not
contacted him, but remembered she was in Florida visiting Harold, who owned a condo near Palm Beach. He
was retired now and lived there full time.

Jonas knew where Jenny lived. After she and Eric had
moved to New York, she had come into the gallery where
Jonas worked on several occasions—though now he had
not seen her in over a year. She had enjoyed talking with
him, he thought, because he was her connection to her

life away from New York. A few times they had gone out for a glass of wine or coffee. During those times she had told him that Eric was out of town on business. But she had come to him only sporadically; months would pass between her visits. Jonas had not been able to determine whether she was happy or miserable with Eric. Their conversations only lasted a certain amount of time and were general. She'd ask him if he were painting landscapes in addition to his portraits. She had told him that she had mentioned him to Eric, and her husband had suggested that Jonas paint her. And he had recalled uneasily how he had been incapable of sketching her several years before, and how instead he had drawn his aunt Belinda. His inability to sketch Jenny had always stayed in his mind like an embarrassing reoccurring dream.

His head now throbbed; he was at a loss. Images of Jenny, a succession of them, rapidly crossed his mind, as if he were watching a film in fast forward—Jenny as a fourteen-year-old girl, bouncing the tennis ball with determination and force against a brown patch of earth on a warm dry day in May; Jenny walking toward him, holding her finger in a page of *Women in Love*, as he stood at the backyard gate separating their homes; Jenny asking him to kiss her before he returned to San Francisco; Jenny refusing to see a movie with him the following spring. His most intense memory was of Jenny walking out of the movie theater clutching Eric's hands, her gaze revealing a dark passion. But most painful of all was the image he had retained of Jenny at her bedroom window, grasping the drapes with each hand, her expression wavering between hope and degradation.

He hastened out of the coffee shop and soon found himself outside the building where Jenny lived. A cold gust of wind brushed against his face and he put on the woolen cap he'd been holding; his hands were red, his gloves were not in his pockets.

When Jenny had told him where she and Eric lived, he had not been certain if she had wanted him to visit. She had not asked him to call first and had said to stop by at any time. Once he had asked if she would like him to come when Eric wasn't there. He had been surprised by his boldness. He'd had a few drinks and his speech was more loose than normal, but he had managed to turn it into a joke. Even still, he was surprised he had been that careless with her. He had not wanted to lose her friendship, as sparing as it was. But she had looked back at him, her gray-brown eyes steady beneath her fine brows, and had said, "It doesn't matter whether Eric is home or away on business."

In response he had barely smiled, less affected then by the alcohol, his sense of irony prevailing, preventing him from comprehending the inference in her words. Instead he had felt at more of a distance from her.

As he looked up at the building, trying to assess which apartment might be hers, he recalled the first time Jenny had come into the gallery. He had not recognized her initially. He'd been working there for a little over a year and was told as he stood in the back studio, painting a portrait of one of his latest clients, that someone was there to see him, a Mrs. Stram. He had not made the connection between Eric's last name and Jenny and was puzzled. He had looked apologetically at his client, and then turned to the person, a young man who worked at the reception desk, and said he would see Mrs. Stram in ten minutes. He had assumed it was a woman who had wanted her portrait painted in order to surprise her husband.

After his client had left, he sat for a moment to compose himself. He had never been comfortable on a first meeting with a potential client. He had felt awkward and unconfident, not certain whether he would be able to please her or him. Expectations were high— clients anticipated a dignified portrait; they wanted to be viewed in an optimistic and strong light. And Jonas had not felt this would be possible with every client. Some people's natures were too dark, and as he himself was not particularly insightful, he was only able to intuit a person's dark side while painting. He could never refute what he felt; he could not make it better. It was surprising he had not been fired. But he had come to realize that not every client saw the darkness that he had seen; they had been pleased by the effect. They had interpreted what he had thought to be darkness as strength and determination and he had been able to heave a sigh of relief on many occasions throughout that first year. But still he would be apprehensive when he first met a client. For he knew there would be a person at one point who would comprehend the truth in his portrait and would be angered by it.

When Jenny had come into his studio, her cheeks had been flushed, her gray-brown eyes flashing. It was a breezy early spring day. To him she was out of context and it wasn't until she said, "Oh, Jonas," and reached out and clasped both of his hands that he knew for certain it was Jenny. It wasn't that she had physically aged—she was nearly twenty-two and had been married for about eighteen months. It was her expression he had not recognized—although she looked her age, her eyes and posture were that of a much older person.

As she held on to his hands, he kissed her on each cheek. "Sit down, Jenny. I did not know you were in New York."

"I've, I mean, *we* have been living here for the last four months. We were in Philadelphia for the first year and then Eric thought for the sake of his business it would be best if he were centered in New York, and we were coming here more and more often. So we decided it would be best if we moved." He thought she sounded breathless and he vaguely wondered if it was from anxiety about seeing him. She soon told him she liked walking about the city and took a long walk nearly every day. Despite himself, his natural skepticism, he could not help but smile as she spoke. He was pleased to see an old friend and to know she was living close by. They exchanged addresses and realized they lived about ten blocks from each other. He was still lonely in New York—it was before he had made a few friends and so he was delighted someone from his hometown was in close proximity to him. At the time he had been traveling home often on weekends to visit his old friends. For the most part those trips had been disappointing.

As he debated whether or not to ask how she had found out that he was living in New York and where he was working, she told him. Crossing her legs and unbuttoning her jacket, she said she had kept up to date about his whereabouts through his mother. She would call Cora every now and again and ask about him. Once she was married, her mother had not approved of her asking about Jonas. With a light smile she told Jonas she had taken it upon herself to call his mother. "I've always felt comfortable with Cora," she said to him as freely as most twenty-two-year-old women would have, but he saw in her eyes a darkness and seriousness that was not in accord with her age.

What had she seen? What had she experienced? Those questions crossed Jonas's mind and, as gratified as he felt at seeing an old friend, he had been uneasy with her as well. He knew she was older than he was in certain ways; she knew things he did not and had experienced them as well. But that first time together he knew not to ask her any probing questions. He had sensed she hoped to drop in to the gallery to see him on occasion. And now as he stood before her building he realized that both had turned out to be true. His conjecture at the time had been practical. She was new to the city and as he himself had been there for only a little over a year, it was still a new enough experience for him to understand how pleasing it was to visit an old friend. And after fourteen months in the city, he had still felt almost as new to it as she had. He had studied her as she looked about his small workplace. Her eyes were steady, her gaze hopeful and ascertaining.

She turned to him and asked, "Do you still paint seascapes? I remember your painting of the seagull hovering above the waves." She uncrossed her legs and bent forward, clasping her hands together. Her posture did not appear natural. But at that point he wondered what was genuine about her. They hadn't had any prolonged contact since she was eighteen, and now that she was nearly twenty-two, he realized how scant his knowledge of her had been. And what did she know of him—what he had experienced over the last three years? The rejections and slight successes? Yet, studying her, he saw that she believed she knew him quite well. It was the confidence in her tone, the way she assessed him as if knowing what he would say next, nearly completing his sentences.

Had nearly five years passed since she had first stepped into his gallery? he now asked himself as he rang the doorbell to her apartment. He saw that Eric's name was still on the tag next to the apartment number.

It had been an early September evening the next time she had come to the gallery. She had walked in a more sprightly way, seeming more her age than when he first saw her. Her eyes were pensive and sad, but her tone was light. "I was just walking by and thought I'd stop in. Eric's out of town for two weeks. Maybe we can have a drink together. Are you almost through for the day?"

Her sudden appearance had caught him off guard. He had not seen her in six months, and it had slipped his mind that she and Eric were living in New York. In that six-month period he had begun a relationship with a woman who often came into the gallery. He felt himself smiling at Jenny with skepticism. Would she only come to see him when Eric was out of town to pass the time, to help with her loneliness in this new city? "I am going out at eight, but we could have a quick drink now," he said.

"So you have a date, Jonas," she had said with a steady smile. He nodded.

"I don't want to interfere," she had responded evenly.

"You aren't. You are an old friend," he had answered with a touch of irony. And now as he looked up at her building he recalled how dismayed he had been when they had parted that evening. He had regretted his slight sarcasm, his distance from her. That had been a little over four years ago. She next appeared the following year, and then a few more times after that. But on those subsequent visits she had been more restrained with him, less familiar.

He now looked up at the building. He didn't think Jenny was in her apartment—maybe she was with her parents or with Eric's mother and father in Trieste. Jonas walked briskly down the front steps and took a right turn, his head down, his hands dug deep inside his pockets. Approaching the corner of the street, he looked up and saw Jenny coming toward him.

Eight

Lost

She did not recognize him at first. He walked quickly, his head lowered, the coldness seeming to enclose him; just before he raised his eyes she perceived it was Jonas. Blood rushed to her face. Her bare hands thrust inside her coat pockets were now suddenly paralyzed by the frosty air. No longer was grief inoculating her from the frigid weather; she was stung by it.

Later, when Jenny would recall that moment, she would try to summon up what it was about Jonas that had convinced her of his identity. She had been in a fog the month following Eric's death; there were times when she would be unaware not only of the date and time, but of the day of the week, the year, and sometimes the city in which she lived. No one could comfort her. She had had no desire to seek or to be comforted. Had it been Jonas's loose walk in contrast to the way he held his shoulders, high and tight, or had it been how he moved his lowered head, as if mulling over a problem he found irritating? What was it that had caused her to step out of her haze and acknowledge him? Or maybe it was because it had been a shockingly cold day and, despite her state, she had been yearning and searching for the warmth of recognition from a familiar face. But what she would most remember was how upon seeing her he had at first stared at her as if she were a mirage, nearly walking past her. There had been an uncharacteristic dreamy quality in his gaze, his face quite pale, as if viewing an apparition of sorts, followed by a fleeting and sharp look of skepticism. Yet soon his expression revealed a submissive regard for her.

After a brief and painful embrace, her cold fingers pressing his jacket, Jenny inclined her head in the direction of her apartment building and said, "Please come in—it is too cold," her words clipped by the frosty air. He nodded and followed her.

She gathered he had heard of Eric's death and that was why he had come—yet she sensed his uncertainty. She wasn't surprised he had not visited her over the years she had lived in New York. When she had invited him to stop by and see her at any time, she assumed he wouldn't have done so because she was married, intuiting that he was careful in that way. At first she had genuinely wanted Eric to meet Jonas, but the timing had never been right. One day when she and Eric were a few blocks from the studio, she had nearly suggested they go in, but had refrained from doing so. Had she been fearful of Eric's reaction—would he have been critical of Jonas? Would he have put on a supercilious air? She would not have been able to bear any of that. And so Jonas had never painted her portrait—Eric had been interested in him doing so but it wasn't something he had thought a great deal about; he had relied on her to remind him.

Those thoughts ran through her mind as she ushered Jonas inside her apartment. She had felt a simple relief in coming upon a familiar face; it had lessened her sorrow, and his presence was a reminder of her life as it had been before she had known Eric. She thought of Jonas's quick and petite mother, Cora, and how her own mother, Johanna, would often confide in her, the puzzlement she had felt as an adolescent at how different their mothers were and how she had secretly yearned for her mother to possess Cora's frankness. Jenny longed to be back in that world, a world she now perceived as innocent.

Jonas sat across from her in a white-cushioned, high-back chair, Eric's favorite; he leaned forward, his hands clasped between his knees. He studied her for a long moment, his gaze serious, mournful, then he looked about the room. She could see he was somewhat impressed by the objects and the artwork. She noticed his eyes lingering over a copy of a Degas done by a promising young artist who painted replicas of the masters to earn a living. It wasn't unusual for her to have moments of clarity like this, but then she would soon be submerged by her own sorrow and guilt. She felt guilty that she was alive and Eric wasn't, she supposed, and understood her guilt was for reasons she was aware of but had yet to digest.

His eyes again on her, he said, his voice careful, slightly edgy, "I don't know what to say, Jenny. It has been a year since I've seen you, and now this." He motioned with his hand and he might have been speaking of the contents of the room as well as Eric's death. But he followed it immediately with words of condolence, not knowing how she must feel, telling her how deeply sorry he was. She followed his expression as he spoke—the arch of his brows, the sharpness of his nose, which always seemed to correlate with his inbred skepticism, the paleness of his skin as if he were still in shock from seeing her. How thin he was, she thought, bringing herself back to reality again—he was like a refreshment. He was refreshing because he was familiar, and she was no longer familiar to herself. She had to look to the outside, to her parents, to her friends, and now to Jonas—they validated her, who she was, who she had been, but not what she had become. They saw the old Jenny, albeit a sad Jenny, one who still to varying degrees elicited their trust.

She stood up and told Jonas it wasn't necessary to express his sadness for her. Inwardly she was frustrated by his attempts at sympathy. She asked him if he'd like something hot to drink; she knew her voice was calm and perhaps too low. He looked up at her and in his eyes was an acknowledgement of what she said, how she felt. He nodded, and she went to the kitchen to make tea.

When she came back into the room, carrying the tray with the pot and cups, she saw that Jonas was not in the chair but was peering at a bronze sculpture of a lynx that stood on top of a side table; his hands on his hips, he gazed down at the work with an expression of both interest and doubt. Was he doubting the quality of the work or her ownership of it? Suddenly he was aware of her presence. He turned toward her and smiled loosely; his tone was neutral. "It's a nice piece," he said. But she didn't believe he really thought it was.

"Eric found it somewhere," she said, hearing the blandness in her voice. "It was before I knew him," she continued, carefully placing the tray on the coffee table. "I don't know the story behind it. I never asked."

He nodded, accepting the cup she gave to him. She purposely did not look at him; her eyes were glued to the cup and his assured hand grasping it. It struck her that though they had known each other for years, they were in a sense strangers. He had no true awareness of what her life had been like with Eric. She had not confided in him those times over the past four or five years she had visited him at the gallery, and he had not revealed to her very much about his own life. She had not told him about her strained relationship with her husband; she had admitted very little even to herself and only once had she berated Eric. She felt pierced by this thought and bit her lip as if in doing so it would help her subdue the pain. It had been one of the last nights of their honeymoon— the night of the Halloween party in Lucerne when she had come upon Arlene. Arlene, her college roommate who had disappeared soon after their short conversation. She had told Jenny she was going to the women's room to refresh her lipstick, but she had not returned. When Arlene had left her, Jenny had looked around but she could no longer see Eric or Arlene's fiancé. She had waited near the table for Arlene to return for nearly a half hour. About forty-five minutes later Eric had come up to her. By that time she was sitting alone in a corner, her thoughts on Arlene, recalling the year they had lived together, whether there had been any signs. . . . Eric was somewhat drunk, unusual for him, and hadn't realized her anger. "I am going to our room now," she had said to him, her voice hostile. He had nodded and said he would join her soon. He did not come until two hours later. She had been pacing for nearly the entire time. Angrily, she watched as he closed the door, his face shaded by the muted light. "You are a liar, Eric," she cried out, raising her clenched fist.

He studied her for a moment and said evenly, "I do not know what you mean, Jenny. I have been with an old friend, a banker from Zurich, who happened to be here. I wanted to spend some time with him, to catch up."

"And this friend of yours," she retorted, "do you know who he is engaged to? My roommate from college. It is bizarre, Eric."

He smiled slowly and said, "What is so bizarre about it? Jenny, your imagination gets carried away. He met her while she was doing a semester abroad. He told me. It is a coincidence."

"I don't believe you," she cried out, louder this time. Then she sharply pounded her fist on the bureau. But he was silent. He had not refuted anything she had said, had not attempted to explain or deny. In his way he had stunted her anger. At that moment it struck her what her marriage would become—it would be up to her whether or not to accept it. For the remainder of their marriage there had been no more outbursts or confrontations on her part or his.

Jonas asked her now if she'd be staying in New York and she barely nodded, reflecting on how within herself and throughout her marriage, she had been harboring a deep resentment toward Eric, one that she had been neither willing nor capable of shaking, yet she had not been able to leave him either, despite knowing their marriage was doomed.

She heard herself say, "I will stay in New York at least until spring, and haven't yet decided what I will do afterward." But even as she spoke those words she could not relate to them—they sounded as if they were another person's plan, another person's words, and she was only experiencing the reverberation of them.

She hoped Jonas would grow restless from her inability to carry on a sustained conversation; she wanted him to leave her alone with her sadness. It was not because the source of her sorrow was what Jonas likely had understood it to be, but because it was the opposite; therefore his presence only confused her.

He rose again, holding the cup in his hand. She wondered if he intended to stay longer. He seemed in no rush to leave; he gave her the sense that he wanted to linger, the way he walked about the room with ease, now standing before a high glass table, picking up one of the wooden sculptures Eric had collected, most of them purchased before she had known him. He'd had a predilection for small wooden sculptures of naked subjects, many of them with expressions she found mystifying, not knowing if she were witnessing asseverations of fervor or horror.

Jonas turned to her. Drawn in by his deep interest and intent, discarding for a moment her pain, she rose and went to him. She realized how much of his growth as an artist she had missed. It was as if he were her child and she had been a parent preoccupied with her own life, her profession, and was suddenly aware now that her offspring was twenty-one, and she had missed the course of his development. Given her state, she regretted as much as she possibly could the superficial and infrequent conversations they had had over the past five years.

She picked up one of the sculptures and handed it to Jonas. It was one of the few of Eric's selections she liked. He had purchased it a year after they had married. They had been staying in the California desert—it was a wooden figure of a Native American woman—and at the time it had brought to her mind the photographs of Edward Curtis. The figure's eyes were nearly closed, lips not quite smiling, finely sculpted beads covering her breasts. Jonas took it in his free hand gingerly, almost lovingly, she thought, his eyes intently gazing at it, his face gleaming. His natural skeptical expression was now erased and in its place was his passion, his need to comprehend how the work had come to be. Quietly she told him where they had found it, and that it was one of the few pieces Eric had purchased since she had known him and that she had encouraged him to do so. After a few minutes, Jonas looked at her, met her gaze, and said, "It is an exquisite work."

"You don't sculpt, do you?" she asked softly, looking away, across the room, toward the window, gazing out at the bleakness of the day, as if confronting the depths of her loneliness. Even with Jonas, someone she had known for some time, she felt it, and maybe because of his presence she was acknowledging it. But nevertheless, it pained her beyond anything she had experienced, even more than those difficult times with Eric, when he had left her in the dark about himself and his activities and she had felt as if she were in an enclosed room with no light, feeling her way to the door. Whenever she thought of those days she'd shiver, her sense of isolation increasing.

"Are you okay, Jenny?" Jonas asked, putting down the figure next to where he had placed his cup. She thought he sounded uneasy, as if he had been hesitant about asking, had not wanted to get too close.

She smiled wearily at him, tepidly noting his anxious look, her eyelids feeling heavy now; it was an effort to fully lift them and directly gaze at Jonas. "I am better than you may think," she answered; she felt a certain freedom in expressing herself in this way, and mildly grateful to him for having given her the opportunity to do so.

"Yes, Jenny, I cannot imagine." She thought his voice sounded somber and restrained. He took her hand, guided her to the sofa as if she were wearing ice skates on solid ground and he flat-heeled shoes. "Maybe you'd like to rest now," he said, his eyes solicitous. And she smiled—that look seemed unlike him, she fleetingly thought. He sat next to her, still holding her hand. He spoke cautiously, "If you need to talk about what happened to Eric, his accident, or of what your life has been like these past eight years, then I am more than willing to listen. I am your friend. I want to know. But if you do not want to speak or are not ready to do so, then I will not pry." When he loosened his grip, she placed her hand on her lap, and saw he was now looking toward the door. He wanted to leave her. Her pulse quickened; she now did not want him to go. Yet at the same time she knew she was not ready to reveal anything to him—it would take a while to do that. Maybe Jonas would be the one she could confide in—he was someone she had known for years and at the same time she did not know him very deeply; he would provide her with a sense of anonymity that might free her to ultimately speak. But deep within, she knew this would not be the place as Eric's imprint, his presence, so to speak, was evident throughout the apartment—from the small wooden figures to certain pieces of furniture he had insisted on buying. Even the colors displayed in the room had been primarily Eric's choices. It had been his money, she had thought at the time, and she had had other things on her mind—should she apply to graduate school or look for a job—but most incessantly she'd pondered her deeply disturbing marriage. In comparison, furniture (cherry wood as opposed to birch), red or white Oriental carpeting, decorations (embroidered versus silk drapes), the large postmodern paintings, devoid of the artistic nuance of a Rothko or a Pollock, that Eric had been drawn to, that she had found cold and satirical—it had all seemed essentially mundane to her then. And so she had left it entirely up to Eric to choose and he had enjoyed doing so. But now here she was—all those things she had not really cared about were facing her, were now her companions of sorts. The only exception was the one wooden figure—the only object she had felt any affinity to because it had reminded her of a Curtis photograph. Jonas seemed to stand out in stark contrast to these remnants of Eric. She understood that Jonas derived comfort from his skepticism. Yet she also discerned that he possessed the gleaming and intent look—unselfconscious on his part—of a painter. She had forgotten or not realized how long and pale his face was, especially now that he no longer wore a mustache.

When she saw him checking the time on his watch, she stood up, felt color rise in her face, and asked, "Do you need to go, Jonas?" The strain and warmth in her voice seemed to swirl around her, engulfing her like an unexpected fog. She looked at him directly and experienced no sense that she was pleading with him as she would have done with Eric. She caught her reflection in the large and ornate mirror on the wall by the foyer and thought that despite her height she looked small and wavering—overwhelmed—in the midst of Eric's objects; the ceiling had never seemed so high, the paintings, each one a large blob of color, never so oppressive, the Oriental carpeting never so intractable. And when she glanced into the mirror again, all she saw was Jonas's reflection and how his shoulders tilted as he turned toward her.

She knew he was uncomfortable, that he found this apartment ostentatious; she could almost read his thoughts. He had only been inspired by a few of the wooden figures; he had appreciated the raw artistry of them, but not of any other object in his sight—the statue of the lynx had been only a curiosity. Everything else in the room created an emptiness within him, she believed—a sense of nothingness—and he needed to extract himself from it. She imagined what Jonas's apartment must be like—small, with clean lines and much light, marginally untidy, a few of his paintings on the wall, perhaps a print of an artist, one whose technique he was presently studying, hanging in his bedroom so that he could gaze at it when he awoke.

His fingers pressed the woolen cap now in his hands. "I will come by again, tomorrow," he said. His voice was sincere, his look mildly apprehensive.

"I need to see you, Jonas." The words cut through her as if originating from an unknown source.

He seemed to freeze, but then said almost breezily, his somberness lifting for that moment, "Until tomorrow."

As they moved toward the door, she asked, "Why don't we meet somewhere else, a place where we will be free to talk?"

He answered, as if it were an afterthought, "Tomorrow is Sunday. I plan to go into the gallery in the morning. Why don't we meet there at one or so?"

When she closed the door behind him, she felt an immense sense of relief. She was a little less sad, a little less guilty—though she knew she never would be free of remorse; it would be there no matter how she rationalized or what she believed. And she did not know how long it would be before she again would be overcome with sorrow. Yet the next time, she thought, when the melancholy overtook her, maybe she would be more hopeful, maybe she'd be able to lift herself out of it or at least attempt to imagine herself doing so.

From her bedroom came the sound of the phone ringing. She knew it was her mother; she called every day at this time, hoping to convince Jenny to go with them to Trieste in April. Her parents would be traveling earlier this year, in the spring, not during the summer. Jenny believed they would retire in Trieste as Eric's parents had. Like Eric's parents they had never adjusted to America. But the United States was home to her—she did not wish to go with her parents in April. And she did not want to see Eric's parents. They didn't completely trust her—she knew that. They believed their son died because she had not loved him enough—she had not been careful. Six weeks before, she had been in Trieste for his funeral. His parents had insisted it take place abroad and she had not had the will to fight them. Selfishly, perhaps, she thought, she had not been opposed to having it there—for when she returned home, it would be as if she were starting her life anew in America.

When she answered the phone, she thought her mother sounded more circumspect than usual—she knew her mother well, and could sense her mood instantaneously. But Johanna did not mention Trieste. Jenny assumed this was because something else was on her mind. She nearly asked her what it was but she did not want to know; she didn't want the hopeful feeling she had derived from Jonas's visit diminished in any way. Before her mother had a chance to ask, Jenny told her she had decided to go to the Caribbean in the spring. Her mother sounded weary in her response, wishing her a good time, hoping she would be traveling with a friend so she wouldn't be too lonely—after all, she was accustomed to Eric's presence. She couldn't imagine how it must be for Jenny. Yet Jenny felt there was something more—she was not convinced of her mother's sadness as she had been on other occasions; at those times she had felt her mother was honestly empathic with her situation in more ways than she would have imagined. Jenny had wondered if her mother had been aware that her marriage to Eric had been quite painful, but had not allowed herself to acknowledge it. This time her mother sounded less heartfelt, not because she wanted to be but because something else was diverting her. Whatever it was, if it was of importance, she would eventually reveal it to Jenny.

When she hung up the phone she realized this was the first time she had admitted to herself that she would not be going with her parents to Trieste in April, that she would take a trip on her own—she would not ask a friend—she needed to be alone in warm and caressing weather. How cold it was now.

When Jenny went to bed that night, before she fell asleep, she thought of the flight home from Zurich after their honeymoon. She and Eric had not had much to say to each other. It seemed as if the years lay before them—it was a stark and barren landscape she had envisioned and she guessed Eric had felt the same, but perhaps in his mind he had peppered it with moments of color and excitement, his sort of excitement. There must have been something of significance about the flight home or she would not be recalling it now. She wasn't certain what it was, she thought, as she drifted off to sleep. But when she awoke in the middle of the night, startled by the sound of a truck passing by outside her apartment, it occurred to her what it was. As they had sat in the plane, drinking coffee after their meal, he had leaned toward Jenny and had picked up her hand. She had noted as always his manicured nails and she had felt a shiver run through her—she had found his hands even more distasteful than she had in the past. But this time Eric had noticed. "Do you despise me that much, Jenny?" he had asked in his level and dispassionate way.

164

When she looked up at him, she had felt tears coming to her eyes. She had not wanted to hate him, but she knew then that she did, that she had ever since she had first encountered him on the beach. She chided herself within for not having followed her instincts. She had fallen in love with him four months later because of her parents, their life during the war—in his subtle way Eric had evoked in her feelings of guilt and sadness. Sitting up in bed, she realized why this memory was so firm in her mind—for though she had believed she was in love with him, even in their most intimate moments, she really had despised him—her passion for him had been one of hate.

She got up from the bed and went to the window. Crossing the dark sky she saw faint light; dawn was beginning to break. She thought of Jonas's visit, concluding that he had been repelled by the apartment—had found it cold and uninspiring. Eric's taste in art and music had not been sophisticated; he preferred light music over jazz—he didn't like too much intricacy. But this was because of where he had come from—his life had been filled with complexity; it was why his taste had been more on the superficial side—that had soothed him more. He would not be pressed to think or feel too deeply. He had married her because of her youth and inexperience; she lacked profundity and any true connection

165

to what her parents or he had experienced. The more she had realized this, the more and more anger she had felt toward him. Eventually she had become indifferent, involved in the life she was beginning to patch together for herself, less concerned about Eric's whereabouts, his activities—and so the accident had occurred and, yes, she had been responsible.

Nine

Restless

When he awoke the next morning, his mind was filled with a myriad of thoughts—both practical and speculative. As he walked the ten blocks from his apartment to the gallery, a light, wet snow began to fall, clinging to his jacket and eyelashes.

He was becoming more and more disgruntled at the gallery. Painting portraits at first had been good training, but now it had become routine. He had begun to liken himself to an author of formulaic fiction, harnessed to a particular brand of writing, unable to develop an independent style.

It was becoming increasingly impossible, he comprehended, to define himself as a painter. Perhaps it was because he was too exacting with his portraits, he concentrated too much on detail and accuracy. While painting the image of one of his clients, he would think of Sargent to incite himself. But his brush did not possess Sargent's psychological acuity. Although he painted with exactitude and his clients generally were pleased, Jonas would be disappointed with the lack of nuance in a portrait. His initial charcoal shadings were penetrating, poignant, and rife with potential, but he had discovered that when he attempted to transform one of those sketches into a portrait painting, something was lost.

He desperately wanted to discover his true form, but he had expended so much energy on the portraits of his clients, he had not been able to accomplish this these past five or so years. And so, as in San Francisco and then at the studio in his mother's home, he had come to a dead end.

From time to time he would think longingly of those days in his mother's basement when he was experimenting with his own style. But eventually it had been more imperative for him to support himself; the money he had saved while working in San Francisco had begun to run out and at thirty years old he had not wanted to depend on his mother's generosity.

Now that he'd be turning thirty-six at the end of January, he was at a crossroads yet again. It had been more simple the other times—it had been effortless to quit his job in San Francisco and become a waiter while working during the day on his paintings. Then, after he had returned to his mother's home and realized he needed to support himself, the goal had been to look for a job as an artist, one that would not be solely for commercial purposes, one where he would be able to foster his craft. Now his goal was more amorphous—he wanted to develop his own style and it seemed that the route he should take to do so was not as clear and explainable as it had been in the other two instances. He supposed he could work less at the gallery, take on fewer clients, but he had always put so much effort into his work that even though he might not take on as many clients, he might easily put more energy into each portrait instead of less. No, he thought, he needed to make a clean break. It was then—because of his mounting restlessness—it struck him that Jenny might be stopping by to see him in the afternoon.

To escape the cold, he went inside a shop. Standing in line, he noticed a couple in front of him who were intently conversing—he could not determine if they were commiserating or angry with each other. It struck him how fury and empathy could be closely aligned. And soon he was ruminating over Jenny's marriage to Eric; it bewildered him. He had no sense of what it must have been like for her—Eric had been so much older than Jenny. When he was in her apartment the previous day, he had tried to imagine Eric there. He recalled how Eric had walked in that casual but insistent way as he had come down the aisle in the movie theater that night, how he had walked as if his chin were his compass. And Jonas had imagined him crossing the living room in his apartment in the same way. He had seemed old and distant to Jonas, and Jenny in turn had appeared beholden to him, adoring of Eric. And then Jonas had tried to conjure Jenny and Eric conversing, how they might have interacted—would she have been assertive with Eric as she had always been with him, or would she have taken on a pleading demeanor similar to how she had appeared with Eric at the movie theater? But despite these attempts, Jonas had been at a loss—he could not fathom anything, could not hold on to any image of the two of them together. All he concluded was that marriage had changed her. She would never again be the Jenny he had known that summer.

As he left the shop with coffee in hand, his thoughts wandered again to what he should do next in his life, how to break away from the gallery, how to support himself and develop his own style at the same time. It was a dilemma, one that he found both hopeless and invigorating. If Jenny was feeling less mournful in a few months and if she was still in New York, he would discuss it with her. He hoped she would be able to experience happiness again. He believed she had always possessed a sense of contentment, something that had invariably eluded him. He had relished watching her sustain her optimism in the face of having to cope with strict parents. They had perceived American life so differently than she had as an eighteen-year-old. Then he remembered seeing her at the window that early morning after he had left San Francisco for good, that commingling in her expression of degradation and hope.

He walked into the gallery and went to the back where his studio was. It was early and no one had yet come in. The gallery wasn't open to the public until the afternoon, and so he was hoping he'd have a quiet morning, touching up the two paintings he was currently working on—one was of an elderly man, who reminded him of an older version of his mother's boyfriend, Harold, the narrow forehead, the round green eyes and the way he smiled, his lips thin, in a sly yet appealing way. There were times when thoughts of Harold would come to mind more often than imaginings of his father. Whenever Jonas realized this, he'd become annoyed with himself, and then impulsively he'd rummage about for the photo of his father he liked best, the one of him with friends in front of the hardware store. He could not clearly see his father's expression, but because of how shadows and light encircled him, it was the photo in which Jonas most comprehended who David was.

The other portrait he was working on was of a young woman, who appeared to lack a sense of curiosity; she appeared disinterested when sitting for him, her thoughts elsewhere, not seeming to care how she would be depicted.

Before he began to work, he thought of Jenny the previous day, how she had been at her best when she had shown him the wooden figure of the Native American woman—it was then, despite her sorrow, that her hopeful nature had been evident in her appreciation of the work. He recalled how she had handled the piece graciously but firmly, her expression studied and resolute. But moments later she had appeared as hazy as she had been since he had come upon her on the street not far from her home.

After reading the article about Eric's death, he had gone promptly—almost without thinking—to her apartment, and yet when he had spotted her walking down the street toward him he had been startled by her presence—he realized that even when he had made his way to her home he had not expected her to be there. He had gone because he had thought it was what he should do. But he had not expected her to be home. Should she not have been with her parents or in Trieste with Eric's, or traveling with a friend? Why be alone at such a time? But she had chosen to stay and in doing so she was augmenting her grief instead of trying to cope with it; she was allowing it to consume her instead of simply facing it straight on. But then again, what did he know about the grief she was experiencing? The only form of grief he had known was for a person he had never met—his father, his parents' marriage, for something that had never existed for him. And at that thought he felt a deep pain. Perhaps his grief was worse than most because it was ongoing and unexplainable; most would not understand why he still clung to it. He would even chide himself from time to time for feeling that way, yet it would return and he'd become caught up in his sorrow for what had not been, before becoming dismayed with himself for sliding back into that sort of thinking. Then he'd sink into his work.

Jenny did not appear until nearly two in the afternoon. Jonas had lost all sense of time and had stayed longer in the studio than he had intended, working on the hands of the young woman, soft and plump in contrast to her thin and agile form.

She knocked twice before he registered there was someone at the door. For a moment he was caught off guard, as if he had been awakened from a deep sleep. He carefully put down his brush and then hurried toward the door, opening it. She stood there looking both hesitant and pleased, he thought, pleased that she had made the effort to come, to get out of that oppressive apartment. Her gaze did not meet his, but wandered about his studio. She went over to the painting of the young woman and stared at it for a long while. "She doesn't seem very happy, does she, Jonas?" she said, not turning away from the painting but studying it all the more, leaning in closer to the canvas. She was wearing blue jeans and a quilted jacket that fell to the middle of her legs, a scarf around her neck that was a deep violet color. He had not before seen her dressed in such a casual way: even the previous day she had worn loose but graceful pants with a silk blouse, the top button undone, a fine gold chain round her neck. But her demeanor, as it had in the past, had not reflected the calmness and serenity of her clothes; instead, there had been much angst in her expression—a lack of focus in her brown-gray eyes, her lids hooded, her cheeks more hollow, her lips appearing flattened instead of full.

Today she was more composed, he noticed, but in her composure there was an anguish that she seemed to be pushing against—her attempts to sound almost too definite in her comment about the painting, in a sense showing him she was fine or would be so shortly.

Now she turned toward him and smiled. "I like your studio, Jonas; it's inviting, and then there is your work," and she motioned with her hand to the two paintings. Again her words sounded forced, not because she was insincere, he thought, closely watching her, but because she was attempting to override her sadness.

"I am glad you have come, Jenny," he said. Her expression suddenly fell as if she were tired, her eyes weary. He supposed she had not slept well.

"It wasn't easy to come to the gallery," she said simply, honestly, her voice soft; she had lost her bravado, he thought.

"Let's leave then," he said, suddenly feeling confined by the studio, the paintings he wasn't really pleased with. It was as if his flaws were on full display. Not only did he not want them to be revealed to her, he didn't want to have to look at them straight on at this moment. He needed a break, and though he was tentative about being with Jenny, her sense of loss and how she was struggling to fight against it, he believed in a more neutral setting they each would be invigorated, perhaps in a trivial way even return to the rapport they had shared years before. But later when he would look back on that day, he would realize how naïve and self-centered he had been; his first thoughts had been on his career, and Jenny and her experience with Eric had only been secondary. He had understood the tragedy of a man passing before his fiftieth birthday, but on the other hand he had believed that after a certain period of mourning Jenny would be ultimately free to live her life. He had been unaware of all the subtleties and complications. His thinking had been superficial at best and may have indirectly caused her more strain than he had intended it to.

They spent most of that Sunday together, stopping in at cafés, visiting different galleries, and then the Metropolitan. They ended up having an early dinner in the restaurant at the museum. Her presence offered him a freedom from his worries and he thought his might have helped deflect her sadness.

They would meet every ten days or so in the same way, saying very little to each other; he hid any concern he had about his future from her. She obviously had no financial worries and he had many—he wasn't certain he wanted to accept any help from her as he knew she would be more than willing to give; money was not a high priority for her, let alone foremost in her mind. She would be the same Jenny, he understood, with or without the financial freedom she now possessed. And at times he longed to be in her position—how he would be able to paint without worry—but he would shake that thought from his mind. He felt greedy thinking in that way. For he was torn between his allegiance to her as an old friend and his need to go forward with his work.

It wasn't until three months later—the end of March—that she spoke of Eric's accident. It was a surprisingly warm day; the trees were still bare but the earth smelled of early spring. A balmy caressing breeze uplifted them as they walked through Central Park. They had not seen each other in three weeks—it had been the longest separation since he had gone to see her the previous December. Two days before she had returned early from a trip to the Caribbean because it had reminded her too much of Eric—she should have chosen to go to a place where she had not been with him; her intention had been to free herself for a week or two from her mourning. That was how she had explained her early return to Jonas.

Each time they had met over the previous three months, he had encouraged her not to be sad. And on that day he had been more adamant about it than usual, his words more forceful. While she was away, he had decided he must make a change himself, and so his intensity with her had to do with his need to spur himself on as well. The reality was that he and Jenny—for different reasons, of course—were each stuck, and he guessed she was aware of it as much as he was.

After strolling through Central Park, they walked down Fifth Avenue, crowded with tourists. Then, suddenly, the sun disappeared behind the clouds and the air became much cooler. He realized they would need to go inside soon. A painting he had recently begun came to mind. He wanted to show it to her; he was curious to hear what she thought of it. After walking another few blocks, he suggested they take a taxi to his apartment, and explained about the painting. She had not been to his apartment before and told him she'd like to see it as well as the painting. She had appeared less sad at first that day, and had seemed more receptive to his words of encouragement than she had in the past. But the more they walked the more she seemed, he thought, to sink back into her mournful self. He thought a trip to his apartment might help her forget; viewing the beginnings of this new painting of his might distract her.

Inside the taxi, she sat next to him, her fists almost clenched, her hands looking cold, and twenty minutes later as he unlocked the door to his apartment she seemed hesitant about going inside. But then she took a deep breath as if to steel herself before following him across the threshold. He noted how she looked about his apartment. Her gaze slid over to the photo of his father and mother on their wedding day; he had framed it and placed it on top of a small table in the corner beneath the window. She walked over to it and picked it up. "It's Cora," she said quietly, gazing down at it. Whenever he heard his mother's name, he'd feel a tug; it was as if he were for that moment no longer the Jonas he had become. He studied Jenny but could not make out her expression—it was almost vacant—yet the way she had sharply lowered her head to study it, how her fingers tightly grasped the frame revealed her intensity. Still her eyes were neither sad nor expectant but eerily dispassionate. She said nothing else, made no reference to his father. It was as if he were only a shadow. Then, as she placed the photo gingerly back on the table, she looked up at him and asked, "What is it you want me to see, Jonas?" Her words, precise and sharp, stung him. He didn't answer her directly. He moved toward the small alcove next to the kitchen where he worked and she followed him. He pointed to the painting he had begun a few months earlier.

"It's not nearly finished—it's just an idea," he said slowly, looking over the painting, forgetting for a moment her tone.

"You have set the figures at a distance; they are not definable, not fully formed and may never be. My guess is it will be up to the viewer to determine who they are. I think I will like it, Jonas."

There was something in her words—supercilious, intellectualized—and he felt suddenly angry. He turned to her and asked, his tone slightly sharper with her than usual, "What happened to Eric, Jenny?"

At first she was restrained. Maybe she'd been waiting for him to ask, he thought, maybe he was the one who'd needed to be ready to hear, maybe it was why she'd cut short her vacation in the Caribbean: she had needed to talk and he was the one she'd wanted to talk to.

Then a look of alarm crossed her face. She was still for a moment, and then as she began to speak, tears slid down her face, her brown-gray eyes darting. "I believe I am responsible for Eric's death."

His heart beat quickly. He didn't touch or attempt to comfort her. "How are you responsible, Jenny?" he asked, his voice stark and honest, almost echoing.

She turned away and soon was sprawled out on his sofa; she had removed her shoes, her head on one arm rest, her feet on the other, her arm dangling, her thumb pressing a tissue into her palm, her fingertips touching the floor. He lay on the rug across from her, his legs out to the side, his head propped up with one hand, and listened as she told him about her marriage to Eric, about how she believed he had had an affair with her roommate from college, and had assumed there were other women as well. He would be warm at one moment and cold at the next. She paused for a while, then said she had fallen in love with him because he'd given her a sense about her parents' life in Trieste during the war—she'd viewed Eric and his family as her mother and father's saviors and so hers as well. She'd felt bonded to Eric because of it, and mature, but soon after they were married it had dawned on her that she had been naïve. She raised her head and looked over at Jonas. "I was filled with illusions, Jonas. I believed I was mature—I was completely fooled, but only I am responsible for that."

His heart pounded as she spoke but he was determined not to reveal to her his anxiety; his expression remained neutral and he did not attempt to interrupt her words. He longed to ask her again about Eric's accident but refrained from doing so.

She talked more about the difficulties in their marriage, how she would stay up at night, wondering how she could extract herself from the situation without hurting her parents or herself, or causing Eric's parents to distrust her and her mother and father—they had aided her parents at a very tragic time; they had, without a doubt, saved them, after all. Eric had had an older brother who had died during the war. Then ruefully she said that Eric had never truly revealed to her what his childhood had been like, and ultimately his reticence had caused her to dislike him even more. After Eric's death, she had promised herself, she said, again looking over at Jonas, that she would discover what had happened to him during the war, but she honestly had no desire to know. She had understood even before she married him that he was a scarred person; she had been drawn to him because of it. It wasn't that she thought she could change him, but that he would be bonded to her because she appreciated his pain, his flaws.

"I began to hate him, Jonas—hate—an emotion I thought was beyond me. But now that I look back on it, I realize it was my illusions about him, about us, that I hated even more."

As she spoke, he was inwardly distraught. Why hadn't she just walked away from the marriage?

Then she added that she and Eric had not been intimate for two or three years. Eric's work was taking up much of his time and he had become concerned about losing clients. The previous fall he had caught an unusual and severe strain of the flu but had insisted on going on a yacht with a client and his friends. "The waters in the Keys were rough, and they had been drinking—though Eric had always been careful about drinking too much, especially when he was with a client. In most situations he had been guarded about drinking because he could become hazy after only one drink; his tolerance had been low. He'd been taking a lot of medicine too. He leaned over the side of the boat, the waves were high and overpowering—he should have been with the others below, not out on the deck. He was swept overboard; it was dark and they could not locate him."

"How is the accident your fault, Jenny?" Jonas asked, his voice meek and awestricken.

"Don't you see I could have prevented it? I could have insisted he not go. I knew how sick he was, but I did not interfere. I drove him to the airport. I let it happen. I knew he was worried about this particular client, and that he was not well enough to go. He was foggy from the medicine. But I did not stop him. I wanted him not to come home."

Jonas did not respond; he watched as she closed her eyes, her face pale. Talking had exhausted her. Within minutes she was asleep. Jonas took a pillow from his bedroom and gingerly placed it beneath her head. His heart heavy, he covered her sleeping form with an extra blanket he found in his closet, then he went to the alcove to work more on the painting.

Ten

A New Year

Her gaze rested drowsily on a tall enamel lamp in the far corner of the room, the muted light emanating from it and the ensuing shadows striking the wall. She heard a clock ticking softly. A few minutes passed before she became aware of the pillow Jonas had placed beneath her head. She pulled the blanket closer, then propped herself up on her elbows; slowly turning her head to the side, she hazily noticed there were no blinds or drapes on the two adjacent windows. It was dark outside. Her first clear thought was that she might be alone. Where was Jonas? Had he disappeared because he had been so disturbed by what she had told him? Was he walking the streets of New York moodily pondering her words? She imagined his loose walk, his head down, his expression edgy, his shoulders high and tense, as he made his way down a crowded street, not far from where she now lay, and she felt a tightening in her throat.

She listened but could not hear the traffic outside. The windows were closed, yet there was not even the diminished sound of horns honking or cars passing below. She found the silence and stillness in Jonas's apartment overwhelming, more so than in her own home the last few months.

But then she sharply remembered, her heart racing, her thoughts turning to the previous November and the horrific quiet of that evening. In the late afternoon, she had received news of Eric's drowning and learned that his remains had been recovered in the early morning hours.

Not hearing her own steps, she had paced about her dome-like living room for what had seemed like hours, not calling his parents or hers. She believed if she withheld the information long enough, it would no longer be true. As she paced, crossing the black-and-white tiles in the foyer, then over the plush Oriental carpeting to the large flat red painting on the far wall and back again, she rationalized that she had not wanted Eric dead; instead she had only wanted him not to come home to her again. At that thought, she sobbed uncontrollably but kept walking, her arms spread out as if welcoming her sorrow.

Eventually, she picked up the phone to place a call to Trieste. Her mother-in-law answered in her sharp and stoic voice, hewn from her days during the war. It was three o'clock in the morning in western Europe. At once she understood what Jenny was attempting to say. Jenny refrained from mentioning, and would never reveal, that Eric had been ill, that he'd been taking medicine that might have caused confusion. She had spoken only of the accident, attempting to comfort his mother in the best way she knew, her hand shaking as she held the receiver to her ear. That had been nearly five months before, but it seemed to her as if it had taken place years and years ago or that it had been a dream, or rather, a nightmare— one from which she had not fully awakened.

Once she had informed Eric's parents, she knew it would not be necessary to call her own. Agitated, she waited by the phone. Finally, it rang. Yes, they had received the news from Eric's parents, and were phoning to let Jenny know they would soon be with her, they would go to the airport, take the shuttle to New York, and would be ringing her doorbell within two to three hours. If they missed the last shuttle, they would drive to New York. She only listened and then put down the phone. Ten minutes later her doorbell rang; it was

Annette, a friend who lived on another floor, her hair unbrushed, her eyes sleepy but mournful. Johanna had called and asked that she stay with Jenny until they arrived.

The weeks following were a blur for Jenny and even to that day the haze had not entirely dissipated—the difference was she was now accustomed to living in this state, and was able to haltingly recall what she had done on a prior day, whom she had spoken with, and, albeit cautiously, had made plans for her trip to the Caribbean. She also had arranged to meet with a friend or Jonas every so many days. But she still could not remember much about those two weeks after Eric's passing. What stood out in her mind, perhaps because it had been most striking for her, was the priest in Trieste who had given the eulogy. Although she knew very little Italian—her parents had spoken this language as well as German on occasions when they had needed to converse privately in Jenny's presence, wanting to prevent her from knowing what they were saying to each other, and she had known Eric to speak only in English—she understood the context of the priest's words, especially when from time to time he'd emphatically pronounce the word *destino*. Her mother, to her right, would shift in her seat whenever he spoke it. But she could not remember much else about that time. Afterward at Eric's parents' home, people she did not know offered their condolences to her in either Italian or German—her mother introducing them to her, her father sitting in a corner, a napkin covering his knees, a glass of wine in his hand, his eyes wide open, his expression alarmed, as she imagined he must have appeared when he first heard the news. Or maybe he had been thinking of the past in Trieste, the war; perhaps seeing certain people he hadn't seen since the war had stirred his memory.

Eric's parents were stunned, yet strong and gracious; his mother, Alma, in her late seventies, was tall and stately with dark hair and blue eyes, the same color as Eric's. Whenever she looked over at Jenny, Jenny would shudder. She thought Alma had not completely trusted her when she had been introduced to her as Eric's fiancée before the wedding. She had been disappointed in Jenny's youth.

The plane ride home was also vague, and she barely remembered staying with her parents until early December, or what she did, where she went. Had old friends from high school stopped by to see her?

On the fifth of the month, her parents had driven her back to New York, then stayed with her for a few days, saying before they left that they would come again at Christmas. But a few weeks later, they both had come down with colds, and so they had not come for the holiday. Jenny did not travel to Boston to see them until the first day of the new year.

During her two-week stay in January, she refrained from telling them that Jonas had come to see her at the end of December and that she would continue to see him. They were still not fully well, and she was uncertain how they would respond to her reconnecting with him.

Whenever she'd walk out of their house, she'd look over at Jonas's old home; the lights would be off and there would be no car in the driveway. When Jenny returned to New York in the middle of the month, Jonas would tell her his mother had been in Florida with Harold.

On afternoons when her parents were resting and the temperature had risen to the mid-thirties, she would walk around her old neighborhood. One day she went to the playground of the school she had attended, remembering how she had not known anyone when she had come from Hartford at the age of fourteen and how alone she had felt, sitting in the car as her mother drove her to school. She went to the very spot where she had stood that day in early spring, her first one there, feeling the warmth of the sun shining down on her, superseding the chill in the air, and how the other students one by one began to approach her. She smiled when she thought of how she had made friends quickly. She had been in the eighth grade and the other students had taken to her almost from the start. It was as if she were a celebrity. In their young minds, Connecticut was the exotic equivalent of New York City or Los Angeles. They'd sensed she was different, but it was a difference that had drawn them to her. By the time she was in high school she was one of them; she was no longer a welcome and mysterious stranger, but a member of their community. She'd kept her parents at a distance from her friends. Most of those students had had no idea about World War II, other than knowing of an uncle who may have gone to battle overseas, or one of their fathers, perhaps, but it was not talked about or discussed. It was always viewed from a distance as if whoever spoke of it was looking through a telescope to see and then speak of the constellations, without any knowledge of the difference between the Big Dipper and Orion. They all had been born in the mid-fifties like herself, when the war was no longer a reality, just a distant occurrence that if not mentioned would be soon forgotten. And even Jonas, whose father had died before being sent off to Europe, did not understand the agony of the war—for it wasn't the war that had caused his father's death, but an illness. She had always been different in that way from her school friends; she had always carried with her an extra burden that no one else seemed to bear. She had experienced the reality of war in her parents' anguished expressions; they were more restive than other parents, more protective, more grounded in a dark reality and so less hopeful, and they spoke with noticeable accents. At one point she began to deny what she was experiencing, convincing herself she was like her friends from school, an American, and only marginally affected by a war that had occurred so many miles away, across what seemed to them an illimitable Atlantic Ocean. But she could only fool herself for so long—as she visited Europe with her parents for a month every other summer, she knew the distance was much shorter than her friends realized or she wanted to acknowledge.

She now heard the apartment door open and she sat up erectly. Another light was switched on and she sharply turned her head. Jonas was coming through the door, carrying two bags filled with groceries, one in each arm.

"I thought I'd make dinner," he said, meeting her gaze, and her first thought was that he seemed unmoved. He appeared no different; he looked at her in the same way, his eyes both objective and sensitive. He had not changed toward her. She was at a loss for words; she was overcome by his acceptance.

"You don't despise me?" she asked, staring at him. He turned away and her eyes followed him as he went toward the kitchen. She heard him placing the bags on the counter. Then within seconds he was standing before her.

"Why should I despise you?" he asked. "Because, understandably, you wanted Eric not to come home?"

Staring up at him, she nodded slowly. Then she stood up, the blanket sliding to the floor, and said, "Jonas, don't be too easy on me."

"Eric's death was an accident. He could just as easily have fallen into the water if he were in perfect health. Unless, if there was foul play involved—someone had pushed him overboard."

She began to shake and then felt the pressure of his hands clasping hers. "People feel responsible when they are close to one who has passed—that's just the way it is; they always find a way because they want to be a part of it as they were part of the person's life," he said.

She felt herself smiling and her trembling begin to subside. His hand felt warm on hers and she felt grateful to him—extremely so. Although she was only an inch shorter than he was, he kissed the top of her head.

"Thank you, Jonas," she said, wrapping her arms around him.

~

Jonas's plainspoken words had moved Eric further from her emotions; in the following days he began to seem more and more at a distance from her, more of a phenomenon of some sort, no longer a person to whom she had been married, but more like a portrait of a well-known historical figure she had seen again and again, a painting that reflected his or her role in history, for good or evil, or both, one whom she could not touch, whose existence she could only imagine. And so her memories of Eric became both circumscribed and unreal. She would recall his appearance on the beach that hot July day, the bright sun illuminating his curly blond-brown hair, the sound of waves crashing against the shore, and how he had said her name that first time, his pronunciation almost lyrical, seemingly guileless. And then how he had shown up in the foyer of her college dorm—how well dressed and sophisticated he had appeared against the backdrop of the college campus— the easy way in which he had unfolded his crossed arms as she approached him, revealing his tie clip, pure gold. But whenever she'd think of their honeymoon, how often he would disappear, and the receding tenderness then near indifference in his lovemaking, her impression of him became harsh—so much so that she needed to stop herself from remembering.

~

Once she moved on to this next phase in her life, she became more aware of those around her. She recognized that her parents were older now, not very old, but her father, she supposed, would be retiring in the next five years or so. Her mother's memory was no longer as sharp as it had been in the past; her father moved with less vigor and was working at the shoe store four days a week instead of five. And in the eyes of her few female friends, she witnessed not only their support of her, for what she had experienced, but how their support of her fatigued them as well. Then there was Jonas—it was now clear to her he was struggling financially and he needed to make a change in his career. She wanted to help him, but she did not know how to offer assistance; she did not know how much his innate pride would come into play. More than anyone else and mostly by his presence alone, he had helped her comprehend the previous eight years.

On a Sunday in mid-June, she and Jonas were walking from the art gallery to a café a few blocks away, one they often frequented. The sun was bright and the air warm and close. Throngs of pedestrians surrounded them. As they approached the café, there were fewer people about. Jenny, feeling relaxed and enlivened, remembered Jonas's latest work. She asked him about the painting he'd been working on, the one she had seen in his apartment a few months before. He hadn't mentioned it since the day he'd brought her to his apartment and shown her the beginnings of this work. He turned to her and said, "I've finished it." His voice was clipped and she wondered if he had been offended she had not asked about it sooner.

In truth, she had not thought about it until that moment. After her revelation to Jonas that day in late March, her efforts had been concentrated on freeing herself from the specter of Eric. She had begun by redecorating her apartment, then spending a long weekend alone in Chicago, a place where she and Eric and not been together. Only of late had she begun to view her parents and friends with her former sense of empathy. She now stopped walking and said simply, "I'd like to see it today." She thought he was deliberating as he did not answer her immediately. Instead he looked away, in the direction of a group of tourists equipped with cameras and shopping bags, coming out of a restaurant across the street, studying them as if expecting to see someone he knew.

Then within moments, he hailed a taxi and they were on their way to his apartment. They didn't speak during the ride. He neglected to explain why he had called out for a cab; they could easily have walked. Had he wanted to get her there before she changed her mind? Or was he impatient to see what her response would be? She looked at him, but he was staring directly forward, as if he were driving the taxi.

He did not look over at her until the driver stopped the car in front of the apartment building. He smiled uncertainly as she got out of the cab. When they walked into his apartment, he motioned for her to sit down and said he would bring the painting to her, but then he hesitated and asked if she would like a glass of wine first.

"Let me see the painting," she said, as she sat back on the sofa, remembering how in that very same spot just a few months before, she had revealed all to him, and she felt uneasy. It had been a turning point in her life but she wasn't convinced she would not be sad again. A sense of freedom had buoyed her after that day. Vaguely, she understood she might be repressing more grief and uncertainty. But she had opted for happiness; she had not wanted to be sad for so long. She was at an important age—it would soon be necessary for her to make decisions about her future with a clear mind.

He carried the painting into the room, then knelt before her, the canvas leaning against his chest, his hands cupping the edges. She noticed how lean and hungry his fingers seemed. It unnerved her. To divert herself, she focused on the painting and was immediately struck because she found it different from his other works. It was both more personal and less personal, closer in perspective and more distant. She leaned closer to it and saw the two figures in the background, leaning against a wooden railing—it seemed from the past at first, from another time, but then she saw it was very much of the present. She could not determine whether or not the figures were male or female, one of each, or both the same. It was not an intimate interaction, but one of warmth and fluidity. At the front of the painting were thick patches of grass and bushes, a lime green color, and the figures were dressed in pants or maybe not—it was difficult to tell. Their forms were partially turned away from the viewer, partly covered by the foliage—all Jenny could see clearly were their profiles, one with a flat look and the other a more prominent one, a Roman nose. It was provocative—not in a seductive way, but more in a thoughtful one. They trusted but did not trust each other. They were both calm and anxious, assured and not confident. It really was a study in contrasts, but it was happening all at once.

She looked up at Jonas and asked, "What were your thoughts when you painted this?"

"Thoughts?" he asked, smiling. "I don't necessarily have thoughts; I see images, have impressions—one leads to the next."

"But your portraits," Jenny began, assuredly.

"Yes, my portraits are filled with thoughts—that is the problem. I think of what each customer wants, how each one wants to be depicted—it is if I am holding my brush wearing handcuffs, painting each circumscribed stroke a subject desires, choosing colors he or she hopes to be portrayed in. Except for the young woman I painted recently—she didn't care, but I felt I was led by her mother, who wanted me to paint her, I think, so she could discover who her daughter was."

"But these figures are not definable at all—I am not even certain of the sex of either of them. Is one a man and one a woman? Are they both men, both women?" Jenny could not take her eyes from the painting. All she wanted was answers—she wanted to know more about Jonas. Who was he? Maybe she was not unlike the young woman's mother, she thought, needing to find out through a painting the reality of a person.

She felt him studying her, and she now looked up from the work to meet his gaze. "It isn't important what sex they are, or who I think they are—it is for the viewer to decide," he said earnestly, his voice devoid of his usual skepticism.

She felt disoriented as he spoke—she had always longed for order. Through this painting he was refuting her sense of structure. It was his view of things, she understood; she had not realized how foreign it was from hers—she had firmly believed, taken for granted, that their perspectives on life were similar.

"So is this the new style you are trying to develop, Jonas?" she asked, gauging his expression, anticipating that at any moment he would return to his old self.

"I don't know, Jenny—I am just playing around with things. But what do you think—does it or does it not work?"

"Does it work?" she asked with intelligent caution. "I don't know—all I can say is, yes, it does work for me." She heard the sincerity in her voice yet while she spoke he looked at her bemusedly.

She watched as he easily stood up and carried the painting back to the alcove; she then heard him placing it on the easel. When he came back to her, he said nonchalantly, as if his thoughts were on other things, "Let's go." She was deeply disappointed; she did not want to go. He appeared intent on leaving. She wondered if he was meeting someone. He was in a hurry—as impatient as he had been to get there, he was as equally restless to leave.

She stood up and began to follow him to the door. Within seconds she stopped; meeting his surprised look, she said, "I don't want to go, Jonas—I want to stay. I believe we have something to accomplish together. I am not certain what it is. I don't want to leave until we know."

Later, when she'd recall that day, what would first occur to her would be the bewildered expression on his face at that moment—it was as if she had unmasked him in some way, had pushed aside the skeptical façade he had worn as protection for so long. And then she'd wonder what had prompted her to speak so directly to him; she had not intended to say a word.

He remained silent; her heart beat erratically. Then he said, "I am not sure what you mean, Jenny, what you are trying to say." He scratched his head, sat down on the sofa.

She guessed he was trying to determine in what way she wanted him. He appeared to be at a loss, and despite her anguish she smiled because she realized she was at as much of a loss as he was. Then he stood up, and as if on cue they both began to pace. There was not much space in his living room, and they soon ran into each other. She could never remember who laughed first, or maybe she cried because she had not wanted to run so quickly from her widowhood. She had not mourned enough, yet she could not prevent whatever was to occur next from happening. She was compelled to not leave Jonas, and was convinced he should not leave her either. She would look back on that day and wonder what had taken hold of her—had it been pure instinct? Had she wanted to release herself from her mourning? Was it because she wanted to help Jonas as she knew she could, support him in his endeavor? But she never would wonder if it was because she had fallen in love with him. After Eric, she had promised herself she would not do so again.

On that mid-June day they decided they would form a partnership, that, yes, they would marry and perhaps would have children, and Jonas would continue to follow his dream of becoming an artist. They passionately liked and, yes, loved each other. They sat up all night talking excitedly about their future together, how they should have realized it years ago, that she should have left Eric once she had connected with Jonas in New York, maybe he would still be alive today if she had, maybe if she had left him, he would have returned to Trieste and carried out his business from there. Jonas interjected and said that was the past and it was best not to relive it; neither she nor Eric should be faulted for their decisions.

When their lips met, she held Jonas by his arms, assertively, firmly. He moved closer to her, his fingers running through her hair.

His strength, she knew, was rooted in his dedication to his work, while hers lay in her ability to reach out to life—hers, and to the lives of those surrounding her. She knew she had embraced her parents' anguish too fully, perhaps, and Eric's as well. Now it was Jonas. But she believed he would provide reciprocity—he had not experienced the darkness her parents and Eric had, and so she was hoping for a fulfillment she had not before known.

After the first few hours of their fervor had passed, Jonas suddenly was quiet. He sprang up in the dark and said he wasn't certain about marriage—he had never really witnessed one in his life—he'd never seen his parents together, and his mother had kept her relationship with Harold at a distance from him. He'd not really lived with another woman before—he had attempted to but had always held on to his own apartment. He really was a novice at all this. She could only see the outline of his form. She got up and went to him. Finding his face, she stroked it and said, "I understand, Jonas but all those things don't really matter. You could say I am as much as a novice as you are. My parents were scarred by the war—I don't think their marriage is a healthy one—and because of his experiences as a child and the age difference between us my marriage to Eric was even more unhealthy. Don't worry, Jonas. We will prevail."

The more she spoke, the more she understood how much he questioned her words.

~

Over the summer that followed, in his free time, Jonas would wander the city streets, trying to convince himself of the purpose of marriage. Other than what she had told him the one time she had spoken of her and Eric's strained relationship and her late husband's accident, Jenny had not revealed more about them as a couple. In his darkest moments Jonas wondered if there was something she was shading from him about her marriage to Eric. Had she donned her mask yet again? He had not the audacity to ask her to lift it.

Recently he'd come across the sketch he had begun of Jenny that had turned out to be Belinda, his aunt. It struck him he'd done the drawing as if he'd been imagining Jenny in a stark light, not through shadow—that had been a mistake, an obvious one, one a novice would make. Surprisingly it had taken him years to realize.

During his walks he'd observe couples, older ones, younger ones, some appearing content, others seeming ill at ease. In doing so he was not attempting as he had in the past to glean what his parents' marriage had been like but instead to conjure what his and Jenny's would become. After each outing he would return to his studio and submerge himself more and more in his work.

~

They were married the following January, the first day of the year. In respect to Eric's passing it was a quiet ceremony. It took place in the afternoon. The reception was held at a restaurant in their hometown, across the road from the ocean, close to where Jenny and Jonas had walked that late August night, prior to his return to San Francisco and before she had left for college.

Later when Jenny would recall their wedding day, she'd think of her father, her very brave father, standing in the lobby of the restaurant, looking out the window at the turbulent sea, then checking his watch, the hostess approaching, asking if he was waiting for someone. And how her mother, while others were up and conversing, had sat alone at the table, her soft, round hands resting on her lap.

There had been something about the expression on Johanna's face that Jenny had not understood, her mother's eyes darting with a hint of suspicion, her lips closed in a half-smile, revealing a piercing sort of love. At that moment Jenny had been possessed with a strong desire to know the truth; she moved toward her mother. But as she began to approach, she felt the warmth of Jonas's fingers running across her shoulder. He whispered into her ear that he wanted to introduce her to an old friend of his, and the intensity of her longing to know more of Johanna dissolved.

They had decided to join their names, and from that day forward, with an ironic expression and a firmer stroke than before, he signed his paintings Jonas Smila-Hoffman. And she, who had not thought the name Smila on its own, or Stram, in any way, had suited her, was pleased with Jenny Smila-Hoffman; it better reflected who she was, shade and light.

Ingram Content Group UK Ltd.
Milton Keynes UK
UKHW012202200323
418888UK00014B/375/J